'A waspishly funny novel' *Daily Express*

'Harshly funny with a squashy centre, a bit like an *Absolutely Fabulous* that you can carry in your handbag' *OK!*

About the Author

Since she graduated in English Literature from Oxford University, Cassandra Brooke has lived a restless and festive life – as an art historian, journalist and critic, lecturer and travel guide, broadcaster, scriptwriter for television and radio, historical novelist, Arts Council committee dragon, and as a campaigner for such worthy causes as the preservation of tropical rain forests, the protection of endangered vultures, and women's membership of Lord's cricket ground. Between these activities Cassandra has lived in France, achieved two marriages, three children and a large house in south-west London. *With Much Love* is the sequel to her first novel, *Dear Venus*, and her third novel, *All My Worldly Goods* will be published next year.

CASSANDRA BROOKE

With Much Love

New York London Toronto Sydney Tokyo Singapore

For Selina

First published in Great Britain by Pocket Books, 1993
An imprint of Simon & Schuster Ltd
A Paramount Communications Company

Simon & Schuster Ltd
West Garden Place
Kendal Street
London W1 2AQ

Simon & Schuster of Australia Pty Ltd
Sydney

A CIP catalogue record for this book is
available from the British Library

ISBN 0–671–85193–4

Typeset by Florencetype Ltd, Kewstoke, Avon
Printed and Bound by
Harper*Collins* Manufacturing,
Glasgow

February

93 Avenida de Cervantes
Madrid
Spain

February 20th

My dear Janice,

Welcome home.

Your phone-call was a surprise from the blue. I'd imagined you gone for ever – in a Bangkok jail, or Chittagong (a trampled postcard reached me from there – where the hell is it?), or else lost to some ethnic wilderness of bells and beads. What on earth is the appeal of those faraway slums where the bed-bugs are free and you can get smashed on coke but can't buy a decent bottle of wine? Enlighten me.

So, there you are, back again in London. Wonderful! Alone, I assume, with the discarded Harry still screwing his way round Washington. Thank heavens you got rid of him at last. And how very brave to have returned to the scene of your own crimes. Do tell me – your lady neighbours in River Mews, did they ever find out about our outrageous bet last year, and what you did to their husbands when they weren't looking? I long to know.

Now I need to tell you why we're here, and not in Greece. Well, in a nutshell – and I'm endeavouring to keep a straight face – our esteemed ambassador in Madrid has been fatally injured in what is officially described as a 'climbing accident' in the Spanish Pyrenees, along with his No 2 who just so happens to have been a rather ripe lady (which puts me in mind of the limerick that ends 'and instead of coming, he went').

As I understand it, the normal practice when such diplomatic irregularities occur is for the First Secretary (No 3 in the hierarchy) to step into the breach *ad interim*, as they say, until such times as a new ambassador can be laundered – in other words someone less likely to become over-eager while screwing his No 2 on a high mountain ledge. In this case, however, the resident First Secretary was enjoying a nervous breakdown and being coaxed towards early retirement via Harley Street. A fluent Spanish-speaker was therefore required urgently in Madrid as temporary Chargé d'Affaires (sic); what was more, he had to be someone with – I quote – 'immaculate credentials and a fine delicacy of touch'. That was supposed to be Piers. He rolled about while telling me this.

So that was the F.O.'s New Year message to First Secretary Piers Conway. As a result it was goodbye to Greece after less than eighteen months; and by the beginning of February – Spain here we come.

And now my husband is as follows: Head of Mission in Madrid, acting Ambassador Extraordinary and Plenipotentiary, trusted representative of our dear Queen, entitled to guard of honour on arrival plus band playing two national anthems plus nineteen-gun salute plus flag of Royal Arms on official car plus obligation to invite all British nationals and entire international diplomatic corps to ghastly junketting on Her Majesty's birthday, April 21st – and, Holy Moses, that's barely two months away.

Enough for now. A fuller account to follow.

Lots of love, and write immediately,

Ruth.

1 River Mews
London W4

February 26th

Dearest Ruth,

To be writing to you after so long – very strange, and very familiar all the same. Old times.

This is a brief one: like you I'm still unwinding, trying to wedge myself back into middle-class London.

It's true: I backpacked the Third World. Made me feel about eighteen – in fact most of my companions *were* about eighteen. No, it didn't broaden my mind, but it did release it. The end with Harry had been so mean and sordid: me in a rage of tears, Harry contrite over and over again. There came a moment when I knew my marriage could go on for ever like this, and I couldn't bear it. All those promises gone, gone, gone. If this was our midday, God help us once the evenings drew in. I walked out. Left him a little note. We'd only been in Washington a couple of months.

You ask me what it's like to be back. Sorry to disappoint you, but remarkably the same really. The Janice Blakemore who went to bed with every man in the street might never have existed. Honestly I don't believe the word can ever have got round. I suspect the men haven't dared confess, and their wives haven't dared enquire. Hear no evil, see no evil; just do it on the quiet. Silence has rolled over the past like a magic carpet; and here I am, still the sweet little blonde who's charming to them all. We're such a perfect little community. No rough winds. Only a few winds of change, which I'll now blow your way. Here are the houses that have been hit in my absence.

My immediate neighbour at No 2 (the soft-porn film director) has been hit by no less than his wife. She turned up from the country, having first parked the children in boarding-school, declaring that her duty lay in looking after poor Kevin, so hard-working and so often alone. Kevin, you may recall, is scarcely ever alone: the path to his front door is worn to a trench with the pretty feet of starlettes, bimbettes, modelettes, just about anyone in fact who's young and shapely and prepared to receive the favours of a rich and famous goat who's also an expert lover (as I can testify). Kevin turned up distraught on my doorstep the day after my return with 'Fuckin' 'ell, darlin', what am I supposed t'do? She's 'ere. She's 'ere t'stay.' I gave him a brandy and a hug. 'Remember your marriage vows, Kevin,' I said laughing. 'Sod the marriage vows,' he spluttered. 'She's 'ad all me worldly goods. I've 'ad cleavin' to 'er body. And I'm buggered if I'm gonna forsake all uvvers.' With which he wandered off forlornly looking like a small boy whose balloon has just burst. Now a terrible silence hangs over the house, but at least the nights are quieter.

Houses 3, 4 and 5: no change to speak of. Paul Bellamy the American actor I ridiculously fell for is never there, and the place seeths with louche faggots. Dr. Angus and dour wife are still grey pillars of the NHS. Roger the historian still peers for rare birds in the reed-beds of the local reservoir: his wife's sober moments are even rarer.

No 6 has changed hands since the general election. Courtenay Gascoigne is now a Labour MP and has moved into his new constituency along with his large wife who writes large novels.

No 7 is Bill the architect with wife Nina of the ever-expanding bosom like a pair of her husband's tower-blocks. She is once again my tennis opponent, and it's becoming daily easier to place the ball where she can't see it. No 8 is Ambrose the portrait-painter R.A. with the X-ray eyes whose portrait of me as the Goddess De-Flora was apparently burnt unceremoniously by wife Louisa in the garden before it could be sent to the Summer Exhibition, thank the Lord. Ambrose has been made to promise never to paint a nude again. Louisa rarely talks to me, and Ambrose is too scared to.

The most powerful wind of change has struck No 9. You may remember Macho Maurice the ad-man and his depressed wife Lottie – she of the downcast eyes. Well, the recession has dealt Maurice's agency a body-blow, and he finds himself transferred to Macclesfield. Now here's the fun of it. To help pay the mortgage under the new straightened circumstances Maurice arranged for a lodger

– an impeccable Scottish gentleman by the name of Bannockburn Macgregor, a descendant of Robert the Bruce, so it was rumoured. Maurice promptly departed for Macclesfield, then abroad on some vital agency mission. Enter Bannockburn Macgregor, not as you might expect from Fife or Aberdeen, but Barbados: all six feet nine inches of him, with a smile like a polished grand piano and a voice that strokes you with dark velvet. Apparently he's a fast bowler recruited by Surrey Cricket Club where he's known as Attila the Gun – a reference to his lethal bowling, though to judge by the remarkable transformation in Lottie his gun may not be his bowling arm.

Finally, a touch of tragi-comedy at No 10. Amanda (Ah-man-dah), Harry's ex-lay-in-residence, took an overdose the day after we departed for Washington. She consumed bottles and bottles of sleeping-pills. Fortunately or unfortunately they were homeopathic – Dr. Angus having refused to prescribe the real stuff – and they had about as much effect as a couple of packets of Smarties. She suffered a mild stomach-ache and many tears. Husband Robert remains devotedly in attendance. Kevin was less than sympathetic when he told me. 'Jesus Christ, I fucked 'er too, but she never tried to kill 'erself fer me.' 'Unfeeling brute,' I replied. 'Yeah,' he said, 'aren't I. Now if it'd been you I'd 'ave slit me froat.' 'Liar,' I told him. 'No, cos I loves yer, see.'

I think he really does. Sometimes I wish I could love him. Do you think I'll ever love anyone again?

But truthfully it's lovely, lovely, lovely to be back. It's home.

Whoops! Just heard an explosion down the road. Must be Attila firing off his gun again.

With much love,

Janice.

British Embassy
Madrid

February 28th

Dear Harry,

I am giving you our new address now that we actually have one – 93 Avenida de Cervantes. Not the Quixotic residence you might suppose.

For God's sake don't enquire what I'm doing here. Sufficient to say that I'm standing in for a late-lamented ambassador who was discovered in curious circumstances at the foot of a ravine, roped to his No 2, a comely lady.

I'm here for the summer at least. The Under Secretary in London hinted at something more prestigious to follow. He probably means Iceland. Ruth may divorce me. I think she already likes it here. An improvement on Athens, upon which she certainly left her mark.

Our first two weeks were in a hotel – hardly the easiest of times. The place looked like a set for *The Man in the Iron Mask*: a suit of armour mounted guard at every turn of the stairs. Ruth swore they were more animated than the hotel staff. One in particular she greeted regularly as we retired to bed. She became intrigued by its iron cod-piece, and fitted a condom on it one evening after a merry soirée held by the Irish Ambassador – a man called O'Leary: you may remember him from Cambridge – Bleary O'Leary. He's still bleary. So was Ruth. She denied having done it in the morning. I wonder who removed the condom.

I can see my wife is going to be her customary diplomatic asset.

Sorry about yours. A lovely girl, I always thought. As your former Best Man, may I say I find it hard to understand why you and Janice couldn't make it together, particularly since you appear to make it happily enough with everyone else. Chemistry, presumably. I don't really know about these things, except that Ruth's chemistry is pretty explosive. I suppose I must be a cold fish in many ways, and maybe that's the only way to cope with being married to Ruth. A cold fish with a sense of humour. Helps with this job too.

I suppose one of these days I may find out what the job is.

How is life in Washington? You must tell me.

As ever,

Yours,

Piers.

March

93 Avenida de Cervantes
Madrid

March 2nd

Dear Janice,

It occurs to me that here I am, Mme Chargé d'Affaires (whose affairs, his or mine?), of impeccable Jewish descent, dumped in a land from which all Jews were forcibly evicted five hundred years ago.

We've now been in this city a month – two weeks in a hotel cluttered with mediaeval armour, since when here on the sixth floor of an apartment creaking with mahogany, a double-bed that would accommodate a modest harem, and a view obliquely over the Gran Via where all life is. (The official residence is only for ambassadors proper. At least we're spared the raising-of-the-flag ceremony.)

It feels as though our world has been stood on its head. And not only metaphorically – Piers' response to Spain has been to take up yoga in the bathroom every morning: an appropriate perspective for a career diplomat, you may say. All the same, male genitals viewed this way up look remarkably like offal and make me laugh, though the maid merely shrieked on her first morning, and left.

So here we go: belongings scarcely unpacked and already I have to find a new maid. Piers retorted that Spain is a Catholic country and should be accustomed to miracles. My riposte was to throw back the bathroom curtains. 'A light to lighten the genitals,' I said sweetly: 'Luke 2, verse 32 – well, sort of' – whereupon Her Britannic Majesty's special envoy to King Juan Carlos grabbed his inverted cock with both hands and toppled into the laundry basket. *He* can bloody well interview the next sloe-eyed Carmen.

I promised you a fuller account of how and why we're here. Well, to begin at the beginning: in the beginning was the word, from none other than the Permanent Under Secretary at the Foreign Office (huff puff), in the form of a summons back from Athens immediately 'for consultations' – First Class! Piers was convinced this was the customary sweetener to disguise instant demotion to some diplomatic *gulag* where the First Secretary's wife might have fewer opportunities to embarrass queen and country. He departed for the airport grimly ('shan't bother about pyjamas: they'll issue me with those things with arrows on them'), muttering all the way in the car that dreadful Athens would very soon seem like the Elysian Fields, and why the hell couldn't I have spared the Israeli Ambassador my Jewish jokes and the French Ambassador my body?

But not at all. The interview at the F.O. was brief and to the point.

'I know you'll do a fine job, Conway.' Then the gin flowed.

And here we are. And what does Piers do now we *are* here? He stands on his head bollock-naked and frightens away the maid.

After that triumph, he now claims to be 'settling in'. The only evidence of activity is a book he's nicked from some library on diplomatic protocol for a Head of Mission, which he reads gloomily and quotes at me from the bathroom. '"Ambassadors are occasionally shot at",' he recounted this morning. 'Not when they're upside-down with their willies at half-mast, they aren't,' I assured him. 'In any case you're only a Chargé d'Affaires, and no one bothers to shoot them unless it's their wives.'

The thought of martyrdom made him abandon his yoga. 'The book also says that wives of Heads of Mission are a classic source of indiscretion,' he went on. 'I wonder if the author was thinking of you.'

There was no doubt what Piers was thinking of. Two days ago the German Ambassador threw a party for a terribly famous painter no one here had ever heard of, called Baselitz, who paints nudes upside-down, don't ask me why. Well of course they reminded me instantly of Piers. But with my sharp eye I noticed that the genitalia in Herr Baselitz's paintings remained unsuspended; clearly the man cheats by painting them the right way up first. So I introduced the celebrated artist to my husband, who was a little sober, and suggested he paint Piers in his yoga stance; then he'd get the anatomy right and wouldn't have to go to the trouble of inverting the picture. Piers wasn't particularly amused and neither was the German Ambassador. I fear my brilliance is a lonely desert flower. Please refresh it with happenings in River Mews.

Now there are questions I need to put to you after so long an absence.

1. What exactly have you been doing these last months since you finally abandoned the roving Harry? You only offered a cliché about 'dropping out' and 'going east'. Surely at thirty-six you were too old for the hippie trail.

2. What will you do now? Your painting career was burgeoning before you and Harry swept off to Washington last autumn: can you revive it?

3. What's become of the fearful and brilliant Clive? The last I heard was that he was performing reckless wonders with both violin and cricket-ball, and hadn't yet been expelled from the Paganini School as he was from his last establishment. What is he now – twelve?

4. More intimately – I want to know about the prevailing mood in your tight little street now that its avenging angel has returned. Are they really still intact, those marriages you trespassed on so skilfully to win your bet with me? And where (now that Harry has lost it) is your heart now? Not I trust in Chittagong – though that may be more exciting than the Avenida de Cervantes, where nothing ever seems to happen except bald men strolling to and from their siestas.

On the other hand, behind those tomb-like doors who knows what tears are shed, or what joys are shared? Madrid is that sort of a city. The question is – shall I like it?

The signs are good so far. The Retiro Gardens show the first stirrings of spring: invisible warblers chortle in the bushes. I remember the place silent with midsummer dust when Piers and I last came here on holiday. I wonder if we shall find a cheap summer retreat to rent in the hills as we did in Greece; then Piers can do his loony English boy-scout act and pootle about in knee-length shorts and binoculars, while I lie topless with a good Rioja and a bad novel. But for how much longer, do you suppose, can my breasts defy gravity without sturdy mechanical aid? Oh then, my neat Botticelli Venus, I shall envy you who have always envied me.

Piers insists I'm not to have an affair with a matador. He won't explain why. I suspect pure prejudice. But in any case I don't fancy having a bull's ear flung at me.

Lots of love, and write soon and often,

Ruth.

1 River Mews
London W4

March 8th

Dearest Ruth,

Now I'm back home and settled in I want to tell you what it was like to be a thirty-six-year-old hippie.

Having left Harry to screw half of Washington, it was suddenly a question of 'what now'? I couldn't come straight back here because the house was let till the end of January. So I had over three months to fill. I might have descended on you in Athens like a rag-doll while you and Piers told me what to do with my life. Or I could have moved in with Kevin who's for-ever begging me to, but the last thing I needed was another entanglement. Or I could have been all brisk and professional, rented a studio apartment and trusted to Bill the architect offering me more murals to paint for stinking-rich oil tycoons.

I decided to drop out instead. I've never done it before, and I wanted to know what it felt like. So I packed a bag and headed east.

I didn't set out to be a hippie. I set out to be alone – a test of independence I suppose – with just a break at Christmas somewhere Clive could join me. Some illusion. Alone I was not. Within five minutes of landing at Bombay I found myself attached to a wandering tribe of youth. It was strangely comforting. Aimlessness is congregational: you become part of a drift of international nomads – in my case their appointed elder statesperson and mascot. They cossetted me as though advanced senility might set in any moment. To them I was a survivor from the age of dinosaurs ('You mean you actually *saw* John Lennon!'). They showed some surprise when I produced hash as we sat on a beach in Goa; but that was nothing to the look on their faces as I began to undress to join them bathing naked. From the way they tried hard not to watch I could see they were expecting horrific Secrets from the Mummies' Tomb. I got a kick out of having a better body than most of the girls, who were either top-heavy or anorexic. Then they upped the stakes by making tremendous displays of promiscuity among themselves. I was intrigued: they were so bad at it. I thought I wouldn't tell them I'd recently screwed every man in my street. Let youth keep its dreams.

Then a strange thing happened: we were waylaid by a fortune-teller — 'Permit the divine powers of the East to lay the truth before you': you know the sort of thing. The kids duly had their palms scrutinised and got the usual garbage – marriage, money, children, overcoming hardships. But when it came to me he gazed at my hand for a long time, then said – 'Oh lady, I see many men, so very many, and much pleasure, oh goodness me.' He looked quite bewildered, but that was nothing compared to the expressions on the kids' faces. They'd never realised they had a closet raver in their midst, and demanded details. So after all I told my tale.

After that they became all shy and confidential, and took to coming up on the quiet to seek advice about jobs or parents or marriage – all the things I thought they'd run away from. I tell you, Ruth, a naked teenager under a palm-tree enquiring about opportunities in television or property development is not a turn-on.

I left them finally in Malaysia, went briefly to Bali (where *everyone* talked about opportunities in television or property development) and joined Clive for Christmas in Singapore, which was surprisingly jolly. He was lovely. Then it was Japan for a couple of weeks (suffocating); finally the last month with old friends in Hong Kong, which I loved; the smell of that harbour will remain in my nostrils for ever.

No affairs. Not one. I did have a rather public last fling in Washington to spite Harry (a leaf out of your book – the Russian Ambassador – Harry said the bastards should never have been given 'very favoured nation' status). Since then it's been Janice the chaste. The hippies were too overawed to ask me, and I rather enjoyed my Mother Superior role.

And so here I am, back in my familiar street of neat

white houses and so many fallen husbands, and it's as though my past has never been. As I told you, respectability has returned to River Mews – re-laid like astroturf. Meanwhile I find myself working again. Bill was overjoyed at my return (the *de luxe* architect at No 7, remember? – my patron). But he looks years older: I was quite shocked. Recession has struck in my absence: no more glitzy penthouses requiring expensive murals by J. Blakemore. He does have one playboy commission for me which will pay the gas bill for a month or so: some Indian polo-player wants a design for a mosaic wall to beautify his swimming pool. Bill and I exchanged glances as he told me. What might a polo-playing rajah want for his pool? Water-polo scenes? Hardly, we agreed. Bill was confident he'd want English rusticana. I said much more likely the Kama Sutra, or one of those steamy oriental gardens with handmaidens bearing sweetmeats to Krishna while he's having it off with Radha for the ten-thousandth time and holding out his member to her as if it was a baton in a relay race. I don't fancy that, however plentiful the rupees. Mock not, Ruth, the *membrum virile* presents problems for an artist. It's not, as it were, 'to hand'. So who might I ask to pose? In my recollection Amanda's husband Robert has the best cock in the street, as well as the least used. But can you imagine asking him? 'Hm . . . Excuse me . . . Could you, er . . . make it stand . . .? Great. Just great. Now hold it. Well, yes, *hold* it, just there while I draw it . . . Only a minute longer, please . . . Oh well, another time perhaps.'

I hope Bill's right and it'll be Shakespeare Country

with swans and wild roses – I've become good at that.

I'm also becoming good at keeping Harry at a distance. I'm refusing alimony; foolish and proud, perhaps, but I want to be independent. At the same time I needle him with little missives explaining that Clive needs a Stradivarius at school. That should keep him on his toes.

Meanwhile the divorce proceeds. It's not easy to say this since you've been telling me to divorce Harry since the day I married him. Did you know he'd even screwed the health visitor who came to see if baby Clive was in safe hands. Well, she certainly left knowing how safe Harry's hands were. I used to wonder why she came round so often: and there I was still in bed. Little did I realise Harry was too. You know, I never worked out whether I loved Harry for being an utter bastard, or in spite of his being one. But I do know that I loved him more than I hated him, even in the worst days and the even worse nights: I wanted to grow closer to him, grow old with him, draw the final curtains with him. I really did. Perhaps he was just the devil I knew – and father to my son (another devil). God, I was so young. What was frightening in the end was the certainty of being alone for perhaps always. You say I'm beautiful and sexy and could find another man just like that (indeed I've proved it). But whenever I meet a man I fall for, he either turns out to be queer or after the first few nights of gorgeous lust I suddenly look at him lying there and realise I'd rather be alone and free to explore somebody else next time.

And yet, when I'm forty – when I'm fifty – will it

still be like that? Or will there come a time when I'll gladly settle for anyone who's just kind and prepared to share my Weetabix, if not my bed?

I can already hear you groan – 'If this is what celibacy does to you, for God's sake go back to being Venus.'

Oh yes. You remember Tom Brand – the hot-shot journalist you once introduced me to years ago. Well, I ran into him at a party. He grows more dangerous with the years: I suppose it's all that 'experience' and all those wives. He has High Risk written all over him. What's tempting is to discover what it is so many women fall for, not what makes them leave him afterwards. He's just been separated from No 5, he told me sadly. 'You must be used to the pain by now, Tom,' I suggested; 'there are so many Mrs Brands scattered across London it's become a brand-name.' He laughed like a child who just can't help spilling egg on his nice clean shirt, and asked me out to lunch. I invited him here instead, half-thinking I might enjoy breaking my fast with him. It's that irresistible nonchalance with which everything he says is a foot in your bedroom door, and everywhere he looks you feel naked.

He arrived bearing champagne and flowers, and proceeded to talk of nothing but you, until by the time the proposition came I was quite off the idea. Do you think he might be a good lover? And why, I wonder, have you never slept with him? Perhaps saying 'No' becomes a habit after a while: not that it's one you've practised a great deal in your life.

So Piers forbids you to have an affair with a matador. Ah well, there are still toreadors and picadors, aren't there?

I may have to make do with Tom: he'd be the bull.

But for the moment it's

Yours in great chastity, and with much love,

Janice.

16c Iffley Street
Hammersmith
London W6

March 9th

Ruth of my brightest dreams,

Piers doesn't open your mail, does he? A truly civilised husband you have: a pity he's so boring.

To the point – I may descend on you shortly, preferably at a time when his lordship is *chargé* with an *affaire* far out of town and you are in a friendlier mood than you were last time. My movements are flexible to suit you, metaphorically speaking: it's the usual Spanish drug-running saga taken out of mothballs whenever the editor wearies of bent vicars and the orgies of unheard-of pop singers. I intend to invent most of it as usual – that's what makes me such a good journalist ('Tom Brand uncovers ten-million-pound heroin trail – Exclusive'), then I shall make up to you in a schmaltzy restaurant I know off the Plaza Mayor.

Do you realise, Oh lady of my life, that I've been making up to you for fifteen years without even a nuzzle into your cleavage in return? I used to say, 'I'll have her by my fortieth birthday'; then it was 'by my fiftieth'. Jesus, keep me waiting much longer and I'll need a guide-dog and a splint.

By the way, my divorce looks like going through next month. It's Sarah – if I may put you right: Georgina was four years ago. You never did have a memory for such things, though I must say if I'd been married to Piers for sixteen years I'd have forgotten his name by now.

I know you're panting to know how I got your address since you pointedly didn't give it to me on the phone. I'll tell you. It was through your delectable friend Janice whom I met at a party. Hadn't set eyes on her for three or four years. She looked younger and more beautiful than ever (she didn't say the same about me) – bronzed and slim from some Far Eastern jaunt and in the company of that loathsome film director-hack, Kevin Vance, who was pissed. 'Why are you with him and not me?' I asked. She laughed and invited me to come and see her in that snotty little street where she lives near the river – not far from me as it happens. And she's *alone*. She gave me one of those lunches which annihilate seduction: raw shreds of sea-anemone plus peculiar salads that looked like a cat's innards, washed down with Malvern water. I told her she should cut out travelling in the Far East. But she was wearing tight jeans and no bra: I made a subtle pass at her – you know how subtle I can be – and the bitch just smiled. 'Tom, fuck off,' she said.

She told me she'd finally walked out on Harry, which didn't surprise me. I bumped into the man in Washington a short while ago, and he was screwing around so miserably I suggested he cheer up and go celibate. He just looked gloomier and steered some bimbo off into the darkness for another round of misery. A little touch of Harry in the night.

And to think he could have had Janice, who used to love him with a devotion I always envied. All I've ever managed to inspire is something much more adhesive – like living in a tin of Golden Syrup. You of course, my sweet but never-cloying love, are precisely what a man of my refined palate needs. So I'll keep trying – wear you down with my chivalry and intellect.

Meanwhile I'm on my own again, in this little box of a flat. London is dotted with lovely houses I used to own, now lived in by ex-wives I pay heavily not to see (none of them ever bloody well re-marry). Here I overlook a superior boys' school: they sing hymns in the morning like a choir of angels, and I say to myself, 'Brand, you sounded like that once.' Now even if I sing in the bath the neighbours complain.

I don't believe I can be growing old gracefully.

See you very soon.

Olé!

Tom.

British Embassy
Madrid

March 10th

Dear Harry,

Your job in Washington sounds enlivening. Having no access to English television I don't see your reports.

But the Second Secretary, recently returned from leave, says you are excellent, which of course I can believe. Perhaps when the US President arrives here for the Euro-conference you'll be joining the cavalcade and I can offer you the hospitality expected of a Chargé d'Affaires.

Concerning which, among the first requests I made on arrival here was for an inventory of the embassy cellar. I'm glad to say the late ambassador's taste extended beyond being roped to his *amour*.

I can claim only one other discovery during my first month as Head of Mission. It is actually something I've been working on for much of my career, but have never before had an opportunity to put it into practice. I shall call it Conway's Law, to be defined as follows: work evaporates once those designated to perform it disappear. To be more specific: I have effectively replaced three men – the ambassador (deceased), his No 2 (ditto), and the First Secretary (ga-ga). Now, the view held by the F.O. is that embassy resources are overstretched, the workload burdensome. Not so. Performing the task of three men, I find there is scarcely any work at all. The reason? Not being an accredited ambassador I am ineligible for his formal duties. These accordingly remain unperformed and – as far as I can see – unlamented. Neither may I carry out the duties customarily delegated to a No 2, there being no No 1 to delegate them. These likewise vanish. As to the First Secretary's tasks, since the man's screw went loose these have been for some time painlessly distributed among the Second and Third Secretaries who are young enough to be keen about futile things, as I suppose I once was.

QED I am supernumerary.

At least, this is how it appears at present. Maybe the system will catch up on me, documents be found which I am qualified to sign, and functions I can no longer be disqualified from attending. Meanwhile, long may Conway's Law prevail.

Yours in the splendour of idleness,

Piers.

93 Avenida de Cervantes
Madrid

March 13th

Dear Tom,

You certainly don't change. Every time you get divorced you ask me to go to bed with you. And every time you remarry you ask me the same thing. In between times you disappear: perhaps that tabloid rag of yours becomes your real love.

Yes of course do come. I'd love to see you. Why don't you make it next month and I can graciously invite you to the Queen's Birthday beano which I'm supposed to be organising, according to Piers. Fuck him: it turns out I have far more work to do than he does – being visited by diplomats' wives. Oh, those wives. I've perfected three topics of conversation: 1) the excellence of Real Madrid Football Club about which they know nothing (nor me); 2) the remarkable resurgence of modern Spanish painting (not true, but I have fun making it up, and anyway their knowledge stumbles about as far as El Greco); 3) the grandeur of the Spanish Imperial Eagle in flight (Piers did see one once – I was asleep). If these rich subjects don't terminate the visits swiftly enough I have one other tea-party crusher up my sleeve – the Roman sewage system into which we all flush our loos to this day: did they not know that? (Remarkably they tend not to because it's not true either.)

So I'm busy. Piers is not. He re-shuffles papers, does yoga and reads. His great discovery is the British Council library. He's determined to become cultured, he says. The trouble with Piers is that he *is* cultured. What he is not – begging your pardon – is 'boring'. He's also good in bed. I'm sure you are too: I'm happy to take your word for it. You must be the first man in history to have been divorced five times for being a great lover.

Yes, Janice seems to be flourishing. I must get her out here. The embassy could do with a mural instead of all those portraits of the Duke of Wellington.

Don't forget the Queen's Birthday. I alas cannot. I wonder if they have take-away paella in Madrid.

As ever,
Ruth.

PS Tonight it's dinner with the Minister of the Interior. The last interior minister I dined with tried to explore mine.

93 Avenida de Cervantes
Madrid

March 15th

Dear Janice,

Well! I have news for you. I'm into *good works.* At last I know what it is to be a lady of position and influence. You may now think of me as Ruth Conway, patroness and benefactor. I was even (wrongly) addressed yesterday as 'Your Excellency'. Now, one thing I have never been in my life is 'excellent'. Even Piers has only used that word of me in deepest sarcasm. Fun – perhaps. Good value – depending on what you value. Presentable – on sober occasions. Even beautiful – at least the French Ambassador in Athens found me so. But excellent – never.

The circumstances. Well, we've now been here roughly six weeks. In that time Piers has discovered to his joy that being only a temporary Head of Diplomatic Mission enables him to sidestep virtually all official ambassadorial engagements. He calls this 'doing a Veronica', which is apparently a bull-fighting term for avoiding getting gored: he demonstrates this in our bedroom by shaking a red bath-towel in front of him and then sliding away from it – not always pretty sight. 'Very clever,' I say, 'but it doesn't seem to apply to me.'

And indeed it doesn't. He may be redundant, but I am most certainly not. Mme Chargé d'Affaires is in terrific demand right across the social spectrum. I now know what it's like to be Princess Di, and am practising my doe look and shy smile in the mirror. I tried it on Piers who promptly asked if the shellfish we had for dinner was upsetting my stomach again. I do have the royal handshake to perfection, however, though I really must remember not to have a glass of wine in the other hand.

Now the 'good works' bit. The other evening we were invited to dine with the Minister of the Interior. With memories of Athens, Piers briefed me carefully. The minister was an important man ('Oh God, Piers, I feel a yawn coming on'), magnificently educated in three continents, president of a bank or two, and loaded with the sort of titles only the Spanish aristocracy manage to acquire. Xavier, Marqués de Trujillo y Toledo was the abbreviated version as I understand it – more familiarly known as Don Xavier. 'What do I call him? Zavvy?' Piers ignored me. It'll be a distinguished gathering, he assured me (God, how dreary my husband can get). 'Cleavage or no cleavage?' I asked. Again he ignored me.

It was *not* a distinguished gathering. It was heavy. Chandeliers. Brilliantined footmen. Silver trays. Everyone clanking with medals. Piers wore some sort of sash that looked as if it should have had bullets slotted into it. The company was mostly geriatric, and the Lowest Common Denominator of six languages appeared to be in-shore fishing rights. My neighbour at dinner was the ambassador from Switzerland which has no sea at all: so he was totally silent. I might have been the salt-cellar. After a while Piers could see I had one of my better moments coming on, and shot me murderous stares across the table. So, no Jewish jokes, not even a comment about our late ambassador's high-altitude fornication. I was exceptionally good. It seems that I'm learning.

Except – sod Piers – I'd gone for deep cleavage: my vivid green silk job, very clingy. Bruce Oldfield: as First Lady I've decided to show the flag ('and a hell of a lot more besides,' muttered Piers darkly as we set off). Well, my rewards were certainly tangible: I was touched up by the Moroccan First Secretary who stank of aftershave and grew so excited that he proceeded to touch up Piers too, which my husband ignored manfully with that public school training of his.

But the real reward was Don Xavier, the Marqués de Everywhere. Absolutely sweet. Cultured down to the cuff-links. 'And what do *you* do?' he enquired as we were drinking coffee. (Christ, it must have been one in the morning by then. These Spanish hours.) 'Take tea with diplomats' wives mostly,' I replied. 'And that' – he leaned forward confidentially over his coffee-cup – 'can be a most unrewarding experience. My wife refuses to play any part in it. She stays in the country. You should meet her. You'd like her – I can tell.'

Now, an old hand like me is quick to recognise that an invitation to visit a government minister's wife means there's unlikely to be an invitation to visit his own bed. I was right. Don Xavier had quite other things in mind for me – namely fund-raising. The cause? You may well ask. It sounds improbable, specially for me, but a favourite project of Don Xavier's, he explained, was to establish a Museum of the Spanish Conquistadors in the province of Extremadura where most of the great *conquistadores* had come from. He had quite a collection of items already, as well as a building – a disused monastery apparently – in the small city of Trujillo (I remembered this was one of the marqués's titles, so he probably owned the entire place). Trujillo was where Pizarro came from, the conqueror of Peru, Xavier went on (did he own Peru as well? I wondered). His own dear wife was chief fund-raiser; 'She's done that sort of thing for a great many years. Wonderful at it. Would I consider helping?' The Victoria and Albert Museum in London had already agreed to an exhibition. The publicity could be invaluable, and here is where my contribution would be beyond price – a lady such as myself in my exalted position, and so gracious, patroness of such an event, etc., etc. He spoke in phrases like that: elegant Old World flattery. 'With the adornment of your presence people will lend, even donate, great things. And money of course. In these days we sometimes need to be vulgar.'

I felt extremely doubtful until he added, with an air of huge majesty, 'After all, Spain and England have between us conquered most of the world at one time or another. A small monument to those achievements would be a joint venture to be proud of, do you not think, my lady?'

How could I refuse? Except that I've never raised a fund in my life.

Xavier then clinched the deal with a piece of acute mind-reading. 'This is my nephew Esteban Pelayo.' And suddenly by my side stood the most heavenly young man I'd seen in years – where had he been all dinner? 'Esteban co-ordinates matters here in Madrid – most successfully. He is in commerce. Useful connections. He will give you any assistance you need.'

And much else should I need it, I hoped, aware suddenly that I had by now drunk a great deal of Don Carlos Primero.

'It'll be a pleasure,' I remember saying. As I was fixing this stranger with a meaningful smile a slurp of brandy fell on to my bosom and began trickling down and down. There was an extraordinary silence while Esteban's eyes followed its course like a pair of torches. I wished it could have been his hands.

'If you'd care to meet my wife I could arrange a car for you,' Don Xavier was saying. The brandy had now taken a plunge out of sight and was evaporating on my bra. 'Any day. It's about three hours. I imagine you'd prefer to drive yourself. You could stay with Estelle. She'd enjoy that.'

I wasn't really taking all this in. Esteban was extremely close, and I was aware that Piers was heavily into saying goodbye. 'Yes, any day,' I echoed blearily. My husband's firm hand was steering my elbow towards the door. 'You only have to say when, dear lady.' 'How terribly kind,' I believe I said. 'And thank you for a wonderful evening.'

Don Xavier was quite impervious to my insistent husband. 'No, it's for me to thank you. I shall phone Estelle tomorrow and tell her the good news. I'll have a car waiting for you whenever you wish.'

'Thank you,' I said again. Esteban had gone. Piers had not. He was cross. 'What on earth do you think you're doing?' he demanded in the taxi. 'Fun-raishing,' I replied, and fell asleep. I suppose he got me home.

Thoughts of Esteban's body disturbed my hangover. The hangover went; the thoughts did not.

'And who was that rather dull young man?' Piers asked when we were on speaking terms again the following evening. Dear lovely Piers, I thought, there are things a classical education never taught you.

Anyway, I'll keep you informed of my new life in good works.

Lots of love,

Ruth.

LONDON W6 1400 HRS MARCH 17
CABLE DESPATCH TO:
RUTH CONWAY 93 AVENIDA
CERVANTES MADRID SPAIN PHUCKING
PHONE PERSONALLY SABOTAGED COS
CEASELESSLY TAPPED EFFING SCOTLAND
YARD SUSPECTING ME DRUGS AGENT STOP
HAVE MANUFACTURED HOT STORY MADRID
COINCIDE QUEENS BIRTHDAY
CELEBRATIONS STOP LUSTFULLY TOM

93 Avenida de Cervantes
Madrid

March 18th

Dear Harry,

Your complaints about White House 'news-speak' fall on deaf ears. I'm a diplomat: I know no other language. Unfortunately Ruth does. At a ministerial dinner the other evening her opinions were as exposed as her bosom. Both became alarmingly inflated when fuelled with Don Carlos Primero. I had to support her up six flights of stairs to our flat. She denies having treated the sleeping occupants of No 93 to an impromptu clerihew about the Bishop of Salamanca. No prizes for guessing the rhyme that followed.

I confess to being a troubled man. I hesitate to seek your advice since your own marriage struck the rocks so violently; nonetheless I should like to unburden some anxieties on you concerning my own. Ruth and I used to argue ferociously and end up in bed. More recently we have argued ferociously and ended up in other people's beds. In Athens Ruth's affair with the French Ambassador was, I fear, more rewarding than mine with my lumpen secretary (I used to have better taste: Ruth used to have worse). So far the waters have been relatively untroubled here; but I sense we are drifting apart. Nothing on the surface, but a tug of currents underneath. This saddens me.

The symptoms on my side are also disturbing. Perhaps you will understand. It's a bookish matter. The British Council here has an admirable library, and

Conway's Law has allowed me ample time to peruse it; also to peruse a young assistant who officiates there. The British Council's red carpet may be Axminster rather than Persian, yet it does tend to get unrolled for H.M.'s Head of Mission, and the lady in question flutters about me most becomingly. I can hear you groan 'Oh no, not cradle-snatching now you've hit forty'; but I fear this may be the case. Pretending to myself that it was in thanks for loyal attention, I took her to lunch. That little bridge crossed, last Sunday I invited her to dinner. Her name is Angelica – aptly so. The young angel has the air of spring about her. The loveliest face. I hardly dare think of her body. She moves like a gazelle. She's just twenty – has drifted here through some uncle in the British Council with whose family she is staying for a number of months. Then what?: she doesn't know. The wide and unknown world. Perhaps it's the air of wonder and anticipation that are so irresistible: an angel with dew on her wings.

It's absurd. It must go no further. I could love her, and that would be the end. Meanwhile the vision of her lights my day. This has never happened to me before. I feel as if I'd been lent a key to the Garden of Eden.

I think Conway's Law has its down-side. Heads of Mission ought not to have time to visit libraries.

Kindly advise a tenderfoot – as a relief from news-speak.

Best wishes,

Piers.

1 River Mews

March 19th

Dearest Ruth,

Your account of the diplomatic evening makes me wonder if Piers isn't beginning to take 'Head of Mission' a bit too solemnly. (Does he feel obliged to adopt only the missionary position, I wonder?) I love Piers dearly as you know, but would His Excellency really prefer an *excellent* wife who buttoned her lip and her bosom and was known everywhere as 'Mr Conway's wife'?

I'm the one who's now having to lead a diplomatic life. Clive has been up to his tricks again. I hoped the change of schools might calm him down a bit, but I'm learning yet another lesson in motherhood – namely that fulfilment of great talent does *not* necessarily civilise the talented. On Easter Sunday Clive treated Westminster Abbey to a bravura rendition of a Mozart sonata which owed more to Monty Python than to Wolfgang Amadeus. I could have killed him. Clive's retort was that the school are forever stressing the importance of technical skill, and that his version demanded a great deal more of that than the original. He didn't seem to understand that this wasn't the point. The Principal put it rather more strongly. I've written him one of my 'injured innocent' letters, and warned Clive that to be expelled from two schools in one year would be stretching independence too far. The boy's not even thirteen. He says he's got five pubic hairs. Precocious little beast.

Your friend Tom Brand is beginning to turn the big

guns on me. The other evening he invited me out to dinner at the Gavroche, which announced his intentions pretty clearly. He obviously thought my dress announced my own intentions equally clearly – which was a half-truth. Starvation is a habit I'd rather like to break. He makes the cool assumption that no woman can possibly expect to find love and happiness without him being the provider of it – which, considering his record, is a bit rich. The Lord provideth: the Lord taketh away! I must say he was looking rather magnificent in his silver-grey Italian suit. Talked all the time about you, of course. I'm sure it's genuine: you're the great prize he never won. At the same time he's one of those men who talk passionately about other women in a way designed to make you wish he'd feel the same about you. A kind of oblique seduction.

At the same time, things have a way of not quite working out with Tom. As we were leaving the restaurant a young actress who'd been putting her small fame to the test all evening greeted him with a meaningful kiss, granting me a 'who the hell's she?' look in passing. 'A friend', Tom explained afterwards, lying. 'A friend indeed, or in deed?', I said. He just laughed, and looked smug. He has a great way of making me not want him just when I've decided I do.

Thought for the day: if I were a man who hadn't made love for as long as I haven't, I'd be worried that I'd forgotten how to do it, or couldn't get it up. I fear – or rejoice – that it won't be Tom's problem. At least it had better not be or I shall be right back in the marketplace.

With lots of love,

Janice.

16c Iffley Street
Hammersmith
London W6

March 20th

Dear Ruthless,

Having failed for fifteen years to win you by my looks, charm, intellect and wealth, let me try jealousy.

I've been wining and dining your lovely friend Janice. She has the body of a sylph and the tongue of an adder. I can't make out whether she's utterly adorable or a complete bitch, but I do know that when those eyes grow suddenly wider and bluer across the wine-glasses I am no longer my own master.

Ah well, so you're not jealous. I also have to admit that the only item of clothing Janice shows the slightest inclination to shed in my company is her watch – which she looks at rather pointedly whenever I make a pass at her.

Ruth, please tell me seriously: since you are permanently shacked up with your diplomatic egghead, do you think Janice is a woman I should pursue? I hesitate to say 'marry' because I've done that so often and in any case you'd only laugh. I know she's at least fifteen years younger than I am (all right twenty), but don't you agree I am rather distinguished in my own disreputable way, and I've had a lot of practice at being a husband. You're forever asking me why I've married so many times, and the answer is simple: I enjoy it. I'm very romantic. When you have a muck-raking job like mine, and are as appallingly good at it as I am, you long to be good at something which has all of a man's heart in it. Where I go wrong is handing it over to the first woman who arrives at a party with a split skirt and smelling of gardenias; and it's always the stupid ones who say 'Yes'. By the time I find out it's too late, and there goes another outraged Mrs Brand hellbent on alimony.

So perhaps the hands-off treatment I'm receiving from Janice is all to the good: I may actually get to know her.

Still not jealous?

As my cable will have warned you, I'm definitely coming to Madrid in three weeks. And if you choose to smell of gardenias I shall not complain. Janice may be lovely, but Ruth is always Ruth – ruthless and leaving me Ruthless. (Do you rate my wit any higher than all my other outstanding qualities?)

What is the most expensive hotel in town? The *Daily Snotrag* will pay. Shall I bring you a Stilton – or whatever cheese Piers specially dislikes?

As ever,

Tom.

93 Avenida de Cervantes
Madrid

March 21st

Dear Janice,

The rain in Spain is living up to its reputation. Madrid is as damp and grey as Manchester. So is my mood. It's partly to do with Piers: he's been in a filthy temper ever since the minister's dinner-party.

Seriously, I don't know what's the matter with him. He's very odd. The male menopause can't strike a man at forty can it? Not even Piers. Totally out of character he's lashed out and bought a sports car (Piers in a sports car!) – a Lotus I think it's called. I said I thought it looked a bit small for the lotus position, or any other position for that matter. But he didn't find that at all funny.

He's also bought a new suit – also out of character. Really quite snappy. Makes his crutch bulge nicely. He didn't even like my saying that. Then he started talking about getting a hair transplant. 'You need a brain transplant,' I told him. And he sulked. He's becoming quite absurd.

Met the gorgeous Esteban again at a party. His eyes undress me across a room: mind you, I was pretty undressed when I first met him, so maybe he was just checking. I agreed to talk to him about fund-raising, and I think that'll be the extent of it for now. Don't feel like an involvement at present: must be catching from you.

More shortly.

With much love,

Ruth.

Later. Even as I went to post this the rain stopped. So I unsealed it to tell you so. I'm sitting in an open-air café drinking wonderful coffee. I've decided I like this city. The spring blossom is bursting in the Retiro Gardens.

1 River Mews

March 24th

My poor dearest Ruth,

After that phone-call I wanted to rush you a letter as swiftly as possible.

I'm trying to remember what you said to me more than a year ago when our situations were reversed. You offered such support and comfort – and anger – and laughter when I needed laughter. You made me feel pretty and wanted. You made me understand what friendship was. And you made me feel there was a tomorrow.

So what can I offer? One thought at least: there are huge differences between me then and you now. Piers loves you. Harry only loved screwing around. Piers has flipped his lid temporarily. Harry never flipped his lid at all: he was always consistent – anything in knickers. Piers will come back. Harry could only bounce back and bounce off again.

Beyond that, what can I say? I made such a mess of my own marriage that I'd never dream of advising you on yours. But you are my dearest friend.

I'll wait to hear from you.

So much love,

Janice.

PS This may not be the moment to tell you, but Clive says he's so 'excited' my divorce is going through. I tell him a divorce is not exactly an exciting event. It turns out he has plans. One is that Harry should marry Madonna. I suggest that Harry's a busy man and may not have got round to asking her yet. His plans for me are even more bizarre. I had to point out that just because I'm an artist it doesn't necessarily mean I'd enjoy being married to David Hockney. For one thing – and how does one put this sort of thing to a twelve-year-old? – 'he has other interests', I said. 'And Andy Warhol', I pointed out, 'is actually dead.'

Clive's also longing to meet our West Indian cricketer Bannockburn Macgregor (Attila the Gun). The man's terribly famous, Clive tells me. He's certainly terribly big, Lottie tells me, blushing. And I guess she must know.

Further River Mews-bulletins at a more appropriate time.

J.

93 Avenida de Cervantes
Madrid

March 24th

Very dear Janice,

What must you have made of my phone-call yesterday evening? Even as I yelled and sobbed down the telephone a voice was whispering inside me – 'Ruth, this really isn't you at all.' I have little idea what I told you; I only remember making a great deal of noise.

I hoped I might be more myself today, but I've just gazed in the mirror and I look dreadful. At least sixty. It's appalling. I feel sick. Let me try to clear my head and tell you what happened.

First – the girl (you see, even now I can't get things in the right order). And yet of course the girl does come first – at least in my mind. I'm obsessed by the little bitch. Cow. Thief. Whore. (Why haven't I got a better vocabulary when I need it?) I'd like to rip her beautiful hair out: I'd like to ruin her pretty face. And I'm sure she's pretty: Oh God, I bet she's so very pretty, Janice. Twenty. Only twenty. Girls shouldn't be allowed to be twenty; or maybe they should be locked away in convents till they've got crows-feet and drooping boobs. Then we'd see if my husband would look at them.

And what can she possibly see in him, a girl like that? He's forty. He's balding. He stands on his head in the bathroom. And being Head of a Diplomatic Mission isn't exactly a turn-on, is it? Why isn't she wetting her knickers over Jason Donovan? It's obscene. He's middle-aged. Shall I tell her he gets piles? Even better, shall I tell her he's crazy about cricket? Oh Janice, I want to know if they've made love. It's agony, but I need to know. I daren't ask Piers because he'd lie, and if he didn't it might be worse. 'She's lovely, and I love her,' he said. That hurt more than anything. The most ordinary of words people use all the time, and when he used them about her I wanted to scream. He looked crestfallen as he said it, as if the whole thing was none of his doing.

What's ridiculous is that we've always had an open marriage. Immensely civilised. We've both of us had affairs – me much more than him, admittedly ('You have erogenous zones like other people have chicken-pox,' Piers said once, and we laughed about it). But it's never been love: that we kept for each other – always. 'She's lovely, and I love her.' How could he? I want to cry. I'm not sure I've got any tears left.

What am I going to do? Perhaps I shall wake up tomorrow and know. I suppose I might just cut it off and pickle it. Then we could sit together when we're old and gaze at it in its jar while we recalled past glories. Or else I could kill him. 'Ambassadors are occasionally shot at' – remember? That would make a good story for Tom Brand, and it would add one more sordid drama to Her Majesty's Mission in Madrid. I wonder – seriously – if there's a jinx on this place. The last ambassador suffered *coitus interruptus* falling off a high ledge in the Pyrenees. His lady No 2 enjoyed the same fate. The First Secretary is in the hands of the little men in white coats. And now the temporary Chargé d'Affaires takes his title literally and falls in love with a long-legged bimbo in the British Council library. I begin to see the black humour of all this. Odd how pain can be funny.

I feel exhausted. It's late. And I never did tell you how it all happened. I think I couldn't bear to. When I listened to Piers it was like a death sentence, and I don't want to die twice.

Right now he'll be having a candlelit dinner with her somewhere, going through those beautiful romantic clichés – gazing into her wide eyes, holding hands, murmuring promises he once made to me. Janice, I can't bear this: I need to do something.

I couldn't go on with this letter last night. I decided to get very drunk. But after one drink I just wanted to sleep. The huge bed is all my own now. Piers slinks into the spare room. I enjoy curling up like a wounded animal in my cave.

Then I heard him come back: you know that special timid way people have of turning the key when they're guilt-ridden – you must have heard it often enough with Harry, though perhaps he never did feel guilty and always came in whistling. I couldn't resist looking at my bedside clock to see what time it was. It was quite early; so he probably hadn't been making love to her. That was a small relief. How one clutches at these tiny humiliating things, hoping they might be significant.

Somehow I slept. I suppose misery is exhausting, or else we just retreat into the blank night. And when I awoke it was daylight. That came as a surprise. I've got through the night, I thought. How did I manage to do that? It can't be quite as tragic as I imagined. And suddenly I was furious. I could feel the anger bubbling up inside me until I wanted to burst. I was sitting bolt upright in bed. What on earth could I do?

I needed a target – something I could strike at and not miss. But what? Then it came to me. The library. That was the seat of iniquity, after all; that was her domain. I had a vision of this long-haired siren. I could see her very clearly – pert breasts, jeans stretched over her bum like clingfilm, all that air between her legs (probably between her ears too), a flash of midriff as she reaches up to the high shelves for books she's never heard of and hands them down to Piers with an Estée Lauder smile. *My* Piers – my legally-wedded husband (Jewish ceremony, Christian blessing, registry office; you can't get more wedded than that). Does she really want him? – *why* does she want him? Or is she just flattered by this suave hot-shot who's done her the wondrous favour of making a move on her? And do they talk about me when they're alone? God, Janice, the thought of him saying all those things other women's husbands have said to me so very many times. 'She doesn't understand me' – all that shit; it's so trite but they *say* it. And they mean it, even if it's only for as long as they're trying to get you into bed. Does she really relish Piers playing the lover? He plays the part so wonderfully well, the bastard. Oh, I bet she relishes it. I can see the pretty child smiling one of those complacent smiles the very young put on when they know they've triumphed over a 'wrinkly' (that's me!).

I knew the first thing I was going to do was to wipe the smile off that unmarked, unlined, adorable face.

I looked up the number of the British Council in the phone-book, then tried to calm the hornets' nest in my stomach before plucking up the courage to ring it. It went on ringing for so long I almost gave up – at least I'd tried. Then there was a voice on the other end. Tremblingly I asked for the library. I'd already prepared two voices, my own if the person answering was Spanish, and a thick '*No le comprendo*' if the answer was a Home Counties 'Library – can I help you?' which would presumably be the girl herself. To my great relief I got a man's voice – '*Buenos dias. Biblioteca.*'

His English wasn't up to much, but I preferred not to trust my Spanish: I had to make quite sure I got it right.

'This is the British Embassy here,' I said confidently. 'I should like to order some books for the Chargé d'Affaires, Señor Conway. Perhaps you could arrange to have them delivered.' '*Si, si, señora*, with pleasure' – he managed this much English OK. Some urgent whispering was going on in the background, and I wondered if he was saying something to the girl. 'Please,' the man went on after a moment or two: 'Yes'. I took a deep breath. 'Anything you may have on two subjects – pornography and paedophilia.' There was a long silence at the other end. I felt like a terrorist who'd just planted a bomb, and wanted to run away. 'Excuse me, say again,' came the voice. 'Pornography and paedophilia,' I repeated more loudly, trying to sound matter-of-fact: 'shall I spell that?' There was another pause, and more whispering; then, 'That is all right, *señora*.' 'As soon as possible,' I added firmly. 'Thank you, *señora*,' I heard him say as I put the phone down.

I sat there for a while thinking about that little bomb ticking away. Do you remember those memoirs I started to write in Greece? *Alas in Wonderland*, I was going to call it. Perhaps it should be *Malice in Wonderland*. But how childish malice is. How childish I was being. I didn't feel proud; just foolish.

That was this morning. It's now five in the evening, and Piers is normally back from the embassy around six. He always used to breeze in so cheerfully: 'How about a drink?' Now he slides in with that cringing tact of his. Good grief, he's got the girl of his dreams (mine too, alas), and he manages to look miserable. He is not a good advertisement for love. Nor am I.

Janice, these are brave times. But am I brave?

Love as always,

Ruth.

1 River Mews

March 28th

Dearest Ruth,

I like to think that even as I write Piers' desk at the embassy is buried under steamy reading matter. Tom, I'm afraid, is more sceptical. In his view the only steamy literature likely to be found in a British Council library is a history of the London and North-Eastern Railway.

I hope he's wrong.

Now – seriously – would you like me to come out to Madrid? I easily could once Clive's Easter holiday is over. I'd do it like a shot. Or can I entice you here – take refuge in this genteel madhouse of a street whose inhabitants you know well even though you've never met them?

If neither, what about going away together for a week? I've always fancied a self-indulgent meander through Burgundy from vineyard to vineyard, taking life and a great deal of wine as it comes. Chambertin. Vosne-Romanée. Beaune. Pommard. Volnay. Montrachet. Pouilly. St. Véran. Fleurie. Moulin-à-Vent. How's that for an itinerary, driving southwards, taking minor roads to avoid being breathalysed; perhaps also taking in St. Amour and Nuits St. Georges if a handsome opportunity presents itself?

Does that make you feel better or worse?

It's an open invitation. Whatever you want. Remember – you're beautiful, clever and immensely resourceful. Within a few weeks Piers won't believe how lucky he is – if you're still around.

Now I'm going to chat for a bit in the hope that you need some harmless entertainment.

Having proudly waived Harry's alimony I'm beginning to wish I hadn't. What affects me most is that Bill's architectural practice has done a nose-dive – his Arabs are pulling out following the Gulf War and the Libyan crisis. He's desperately bidding for a new housing estate in Basingstoke, but even if he gets it I can't see Hampshire County Council insisting on murals of Shakespeare Country in every 12' by 10', can you? For the time-being my Indian polo-player's swimming-pool will keep me afloat. No Kama Sutra, you'll be relieved to hear. He's discovered David Hockney and wants 'a bigger splash' with Californian palms. So, this afternoon it'll be Kew Gardens with my sketch-pad. The question is, does he want me to include a reclining boy *à la* Hockney? I find it hard to ask, not knowing his predilections. Kevin advises 'Go for it darlin'. Of course ee's bent – and black. Why don't you get Attila the Gun to pose? Bet that'd make an even bigger splash.'

Talking of whom, Lottie came and confessed all. I was right about the weapon: Attila clearly likes older women. He's supposed to be in strict training for the cricket season. Lottie blushed to tell me how athletic he was, but was worried – the good-hearted creature – that his exercises might not be quite what Surrey Cricket Club had in mind when they signed on a 6ft 9ins West Indian fast bowler. 'Is the 6ft 9 proportional?' I enquired (after all, it's what everyone wants to know, isn't it?); but Lottie either didn't understand or pretended not to. It's extremely difficult listening to confessions from women who are longing to tell you what they're ashamed to tell. Her face, however, tells most things. Maurice in Macclesfield, and she's having the time of her life – probably for the first time in her life. I feel very aunt-like.

Bill and Nina gave a drinks party yesterday for the newcomers at No 6, the Crawleys. Everyone was there – '*toute la rue*' as Ah-man-dah put it. She's become huge since the failed suicide bid. Kevin says it must be the effect of all those homeopathic sleeping pills she took. It's terrible how unkind we are about her. 'Hypocrite,' Kevin accused me. 'After all she nicked yer 'usband. Who the fuckin' 'ell can I persuade to nick my wife? It's drivin' me bananas bein' married.' The Crawleys overheard him and looked appalled; even more so when he added 'You an' I 'aven't 'ad it off since before your 'Arry left. It's criminal.' Soon afterwards the Crawleys broke off talking to the Rev Hope and introduced themselves to me as though I was clearly in need of care and attention. They probably think I've got AIDS. They probably think anyone who has sex has got AIDS. Kevin, who'd taken the 'drinks' invitation to heart by now, made it worse by chipping in with, 'Sexiest little piece in the street, don't you think, Mr. Creepy?' I don't know if he deliberately got the name wrong, but from now on they're 'the Creepy Crawleys'. He smiles all the time and nods like one of those acrylic dogs you see inside car rear-windows. She looks like a faded poster for moral rearmament. They promised to visit me: oh dear! Rescuers to the manner born.

When I'm alone I'm so thankful I've rescued myself.

Tom, needless to say, is convinced that no woman

can consider herself rescued without the benefit of his cock.

And on that note I shall leave you – and long to hear from you.

With great love,

Janice.

Palacio Pizarro
Trujillo
Extremadura
Spain

March 30th

Dear Janice,

I've fled.

Without a word to Piers I just pissed off. The above address is my sanctuary for a few days – *chez* the extraordinary Estelle, wife of the Interior Minister I met a few weeks ago, Don Xavier. Remember? She of fund-raising fame; and – Jesus – I can see why. Estelle is unique. And a friend in need. I shall tell you all.

After yet another sleepless night sticking pins into a silicone model of Piers' bimbo I phoned Xavier, as he had suggested. I tried not to sound fraught; said how keen I was to help with fund-raising for his museum. He was thrilled, he said. Of course I must stay with his wife – I'd love it – she'd love it. Christ, there was so much love flying around I felt I should ask if Piers and his mistress could come too.

'Today?' he said. 'Now? You mean that? Wonderful. I'll ring Estelle.'

Within ten minutes he was back on the phone. There was no problem. I was expected in Trujillo for lunch. A three-hour drive: he'd have a car sent round for me rightaway. He was so very pleased. He'd told Estelle all about me.

I wondered what he had told Estelle. Such a discreet man, Xavier. But I am not.

At ten o'clock sharp there the car was. The man who rang the doorbell was the minister's private secretary, he explained self-importantly. He had a note for me. It was in Xavier's own hand, giving me directions to Trujillo, how to find the house. (House! Just look at the address above!) Estelle would be waiting. She was delighted, he said. Stay a few nights, as many as I wanted.

It sounded just what I needed. I felt better at the very thought of it.

Xavier's secretary took my bag, handed me the car-keys and pointed to an open-top Mercedes – dazzling white. Beads of water still clung to it: the minions had been at work. 'With the minister's compliments, Your Excellency,' the mandarin said. He saluted, opened the door, saluted again and strode away. A map was laid open on the passenger seat. Music tapes were neatly ranked near the stereo: one of them was Elgar's Cello Concerto, I noticed. It looked new. Was nothing overlooked for the British First Lady?

And off I went through the bedlam of Madrid into the dusty countryside.

A button slid the roof down. Another button played

me music. I let the miles roll by. Travel began to wash some of the rubbish from my system, turn my thoughts outwards. Extremadura – I don't know if you've ever been here, but it's Spain's Empty Quarter. Plains. Distant hills. More plains. More distant hills. Black cattle grazing among gigantic thistles. Mile upon mile of evergreen oaks planted out like green umbrellas. Spring flowers were splashed beside the road and across the fields of young corn. It was beautiful. I'd forgotten I could respond; I'd imagined beauty to be something that belonged to my husband's mistress. My spirits began to soar in all this space. And what the hell was I doing here? Fund-raising – in a brand-new open-top ministerial limousine! I loved the feel of the wind on my face, and felt a truant. I love adventures: the not knowing, the never knowing. Piers does not, by the way. Everything has to be prescribed. That's probably why he gets piles.

I glanced at the note from Xavier. 'Palacio Pizarro', it said. 'Climb the hill above the town. You can't miss it.' He was right. A sign read 'Castillo'. Ancient cobbles. Wallflowers sprouting among the rubble of ruined buildings. A green lizard. Far down below lay the Plaza Mayor. I could see storks nesting on every pinnacle, regurgitating disgusting things and clattering their bills (I was reminded of diplomatic dinners in North Yemen). I stopped the car because there was nothing ahead except a massive wall, complete with battlements, a portcullis and a gate that would have dwarfed the Trojan Horse. It seemed I must have arrived.

The man who heaved open the gate stared at this wild-haired witch and said 'The *marquésa* is expecting you.'

I drove into the Middle Ages over a crunch of raked gravel.

Phew!

Janice, I need to de-mystify you. It's actually early morning and I'm writing this by the dark-tower window of my bedroom which is a key-hole overlooking all Extremadura. I doubt if anyone's going to rise in this place for an hour at least, so I shall now tell you about yesterday and how it came about that I forgot to call Piers until he was asleep and furious and had already alerted the police and probably the armed forces. 'You cannot do this to me,' he gobbled over the phone. 'Sorry Piers, I just have, you bastard.'

Xavier had assured me I'd like Estelle. What he didn't say was that she was actually *three* people! I met them in the following order: the late Duchess of Windsor in the morning; Mae West in the evening; Catherine the Great at night. (Nobody in the afternoon – deep siesta.)

She welcomed me on the terrace. Age fifty-ish – who can tell with women in an advanced state of preservation? Actually French, it turned out. Spoke perfect English. Beautiful if you like white porcelain. Face lifted, then lifted again: I could tell that. Slim as an eel. A sheath of a dress. Incredible legs – I gasped. Bracelets clanking. The most formal of greetings. ('My husband has told me about you': that sort of stuff.) After I'd tidied up in my dark tower a handsome gypsy-looking young man in black and white served us cocktails in a formal garden watered by one of those sputtering sprinklers that squirt you in the bum when you aren't looking. We sat, and Estelle began to talk of elegant things – and finally of fund-raising – her life working for Children in Need all over the world. She had the French *Légion d'Honneur* for it, she mentioned casually. The museum was more of a retirement job, something she did for Xavier. All this time I was decorum itself, and nodded diplomatically from time to time. Oh, you'd have been proud of me, Janice. It was hot in the sun – even in March. Summer takes winter by surprise here and kills it stone-dead. We ate delicious fish salads, sipped Marqués de Cácares ('a cousin'), and admired the view ('most of it ours'). Then she explained how useful I might be ('a representative of foreign royalty can oil so many wheels, my dear: alas, my own ancestors were dethroned in the eighteenth century'). Finally she rose for her siesta ('I trust your bed is comfortable. Maria Callas used to complain it was too soft, but you know what Maria was like.').

I'm not normally in awe, but I confess I wasn't entirely looking forward to the evening. I'd seen the Duchess of Windsor performance. I had no idea of the Mae West she was to become.

By the late afternoon the *palacio* was still silent, so I explored the town – very pretty – sipped *limon granizado* in a café, and gazed at the storks on the roofs around. Already the little bimbo seemed a long way away. By the time I returned it was growing dusk. A creaking retainer explained that the *marquésa* was by the pool ('a heated pool', I remembered). She was actually *in* the pool, together with the young man who'd served us drinks before lunch. 'Ah, there you are,' she called out. 'I won't ask you to join us: I'll join you.' And she climbed out. She was entirely naked. In the half-light she could have passed for thirty. 'I always enjoy a little dip with Luis in the evening,' she said wrapping herself in a towel. 'He'll bring us drinks when he's dressed, but he's rather nice like that, don't you think?'

Luis had climbed out, less naked than the *marquésa* by a whisker: he was wearing a sort of G-string. 'Looks a bit like a tea-bag, doesn't it?' she said nonchalantly. 'I assure you it's not.'

I was too stunned by the transformation in Estelle to say anything at all. Could it possibly be the same woman? I peered closely in the dusk to make sure. Curled up deeply in her towel, Estelle hummed contentedly. 'I love it here,' she said after a while. 'The peace. Too hot in the high summer of course. We have an indoor pool. Luis prefers it – don't you Luis?' she said in Spanish. The beautiful young man had returned, immaculate again in black and white, and was pouring out wine. It was almost dark. He lit a lantern and placed it carefully between us. 'Xavier calls him my toy-boy,' she added thoughtfully. 'Personally I wouldn't call what he has a "toy" . . . Oh, don't worry, my dear. He speaks no English.'

Estelle drained her glass of wine. Luis immediately refilled it. Then she waved him away. 'You know,' she went on, 'it's one of the privileges of the old to give employment to the young.' I could hear her let out a little laugh. Then she reached over and touched my arm. 'I think I rather like you. We shall be able to talk.' I hadn't spoken a word.

We dined late that evening – Luis in attendance again. 'Does Xavier mind?', I enquired carefully, a little apprehensive in case Estelle suddenly reverted to being Duchess of Windsor. 'No, no, no,' she said. 'Xavier's a dear man, but a capon. He used to manage it a few times a year, usually on saints' days. But since he turned fifty the only thing he's ever got up is the political ladder. That's a long time to be limp, isn't it? He does have good taste in wine though, doesn't he?' And she motioned to Luis.

Mellowed by Xavier's vintages Estelle began to unfold fragments of her life. She'd married at eighteen ('Arranged of course. A Balkan prince. Can't remember his name. Not much more than a splendid title in uniform.'). The marriage lasted less time than it took to produce a son. Now she has grandchildren, whom she adores. She'd gone into charity work out of boredom and because she seemed fit for nothing else. 'I was hopeless at raising money: I always had too much of my own.' The futility of it all depressed her. She took to sleeping late, drinking late, filling the day with long baths. She even made her charity appeals from the bath.

And that was how it all began, she said. Presidents of banks, magnates, captains of industry: when she managed to get through to them ('my title always helped') they'd enquire about the sound of water. 'I'm in the bath,' she'd explain. It turned them on no end. Suddenly the money poured in as fast as the water poured out. Offers of marriage too, as well as propositions of a less formal kind. 'Oh, I became a tremendous success. I raised millions for children that way in six continents. In England don't you have an Order of the Bath? No one deserved it more than me. But I had to make do with the *Légion d'Honneur*.'

'A word of advice about fund-raising,' she said finally, patting my hand as if I was a little girl. 'It doesn't matter what the cause is – helping children or building up a museum – getting money out of people is always the same: you need to persuade them that you're doing them a huge favour, and be prepared to bestow one yourself when necessary. That's how I married Xavier. It wasn't a favour I had to repeat very often.'

After dinner we sat by the fire until the small hours. The joy of being with Estelle is that she assumes I'm as much a free spirit as she is – which makes me feel it might be true. I can imagine her telling an invading army to 'Fuck off', and they would. Probably bring her champagne.

'And now I want to hear about you,' she announced suddenly. 'Well, for a start,' I said, 'I've just run away from my husband.' Estelle merely nodded: 'What a very sensible thing to do. For good?' I'd never actually thought of that, and felt quite horrified. I said I hoped not; besides I had duties as the Chargé d'Affaires' wife. Estelle looked appalled. 'Nonsense, there are plenty of people capable of making the sandwiches. You should do as you like.'

So I told her about Piers and his little tweetie-pie. I hoped it was too dark for her to see the tears on my face. Estelle sat there gazing into the fire, her long fingers tapping against each other like chopsticks. Eventually she turned to me with a puzzled expression. 'That word "love", it perplexes me,' she said. 'It means so many different things, doesn't it? I've given and received a great deal of love in my time, but it has never occurred to me that my husband should be the instrument of it. For me marriage is a contract, as one might have with a lawyer or a builder: it is for the sake of security in an insecure world, and for the implementation of practical needs. A loyal partnership, if you like. I would never expect to form a "relationship" with my builder or my lawyer, or (as in your case) with a diplomat. So, I feel for you most deeply, my dear, but I am at a disadvantage. I need to give it much thought – and I shall. But now, if you will forgive me.'

She reached out and rang a small hand-bell. Luis appeared, and she took his hand very gently. 'Love,' she said: 'how wonderful and how sad. Nowadays I'm the one who pays out, and soon I suppose I shall be too old for that. You see, I may be Estelle, but I'm a falling star. How fortunate you are to be young.'

I hadn't thought of myself as young for a long time.

She was looking up at Luis fondly. 'The great thing about Spaniards is that they live for the night. It's only we northerners who are taught it's for sleeping.' Then she rose on his arm. 'Good-night, my dear Ruth. I promise to dwell on your predicament, and to find the answer. I'm sure it will prove quite simple. I shall let you know. Meanwhile, don't be too early tomorrow. I'm not at my best in the morning. Before long it won't be just the morning.'

And so she retired in her third role – as Catherine the Great.

I heard the clock strike three. I managed a few hours' sleep before the sun woke me. Now it's high and the place is still quiet. Storks flap to and fro outside my window. Tomorrow I'll drive back to Madrid and face my husband. My wrath against his. He took a mistress without my permission, so I fucked off without his.

Why do I tell you all this? Do you think I'm at a crossroads in my life? Will I be like Estelle in twenty years; and Piers like Xavier, climbing his ladder higher and further away from me? I feel the cool shadow of middle-age.

Oh sod it! Maybe I could just do with Attila the Gun. Your letters cheer me. You're better at being alone than I am at being married. As for the importuning Tom Brand – yes, he wrote to me; even admitted he'd made a pass at you. You find him dangerous. I suppose he is. I'm sure he *would* make you a good lover, for as long as it lasted. Then you'd simply join the long row of XXXXs – in a manner of speaking.

Being back in River Mews must be like returning to Verdun. Each house should have a stone cross in the front-garden: '. . . fell in action Nov. 16th . . . Jan 8th . . . March 22nd . . . April 21st.' (No, not April 21st, heaven preserve us, that's the Queen's birthday and I have to organise the bun-fight.) That *and* Piers in love with tweetie-pie – it's too much.

But I do have an open-top Mercedes, at least for today.

Lots of love,

Ruth.

April

Palacio Pizarro
Trujillo

April 2nd

Dear Ruth Conway,

I do not usually thank my guests for thanking me, but I so greatly enjoyed your company and the smallest excuse to say so will do. By the way, years of fund-raising have left me with a distaste for telephones, which is why I am writing. Whenever you phone you will find me hostile and monosyllabic. Don't be put off. In retrospect I'm pleased.

I enjoy relationships with women so much more than with men. A man either imposes his anatomy or his cheque-book – both delightful but of short duration. With women one can expand and talk of things that really matter, even if what really matters is frequently – men.

We talked a great deal about marriage, as I recall: this I found refreshing since marriage is not a subject I have given much thought to. I have always considered it to be something one either did or did not have, and it didn't make much difference to one's life which. My own experiences may not be typical. My first marriage was at eighteen. He took my virginity: I took my leave soon after. *La permission anglaise* as we say. My second was at thirty-five. I took his title, and he took *his* leave – not quite so soon after, but then Spain is more conservative than France in these matters. The difference too was that, being older and more experienced, Xavier and I remain the best of friends – at a proper distance.

I am still wrestling with the problem you presented to me during our delightful evening. Unfortunately, as I believe I explained, it is not one that has ever confronted me personally. I imagine that both my first husband, whose name I forget, and dear Xavier in their time became enamoured of other women – that would only be natural: what man has not?

But your own predicament is unfamiliar to me since – for reasons I only partly understand – you actually live with your husband. As you know, I have never found it congenial to do such a thing: for me co-habitation is not what marriage is about. In my view *la gamme d'amour* is too wide and wild a universe to spin around a single man. Lovers are like space travellers speeding from star to star. We are weightless; otherwise how could we bear the subterfuges we indulge or the sins we commit? You cannot put love on a collar and lead and command 'Heel!', as you English are so fond of doing with your dogs – perhaps that is why.

The only love worth having is unbound. And sooner or later of course it flies away. That is the joy and the pain of it.

I have to try to imagine what it must be like seen through your eyes. So let me attempt to define this problem of yours.

If you are still sleeping with your husband (not a habit I ever acquired), then what we are concerned with is sexual rivalry, is it not? I can envisage a situation of that kind with a lover, and I am trying to think how I would act. I believe I would have to assume he had grown weary of my body, and I would therefore swiftly obtain a new lover who was not. (This may not be helpful, but you need to remember that I am French, and we are not like you English: we separate out our needs and feelings more easily.)

But if sex is not the primary issue then the 'betrayal', as you have put it, has to be of a more domestic and social kind. A betrayal of companionship. I can certainly imagine being betrayed by a member of my family, or my servants, or a close friend. This would not only be painful, it would also be less easy to resolve since new friends or new members of the family do not arrive every day, and new servants have become lamentably difficult to find. But you are an intelligent woman: a little patience and I am certain a new companion will present himself. Men are so very easy to find. My nephew Esteban, for instance, finds you entirely irresistible. He is a tedious young man, as men of commerce tend to be, though that scarcely enters into it. If he were not my nephew I should have made him my lover; but even I draw a line at incest. You might find him nourishing if you were in the mood. I guarantee he would not disturb your 'relationship' with your husband (who I do not think I would like much). Besides, Esteban has a *fiancée*, poor girl. I have tried to warn her, but she is too stupid. Oh, the Spaniards; how they cherish these sanctimonious bonds.

I sense that I may still be failing to touch the heart of your predicament, and if that is so I can only once again plead ignorance of the nature of it. I did, it is true, once form an attachment to a most handsome gentleman who abandoned me for a well-built chorus-girl: but that was a special case since he was king of some Scandinavian nation, and I have always been a respecter of rank. Besides, he had a wife – the queen presumably. No – the comparison will not help you.

In any case, nowadays I am past these dangerous frolics. Tastes remain, but appetites diminish: I ask only for men to be beautiful and incoherent. It's my women friends who I need to be clever. And *you* are clever, my dear: beautiful too, but that is a purely aesthetic bonus.

So, let us please meet again soon and talk further. I should enjoy that. Come and stay longer. Bring your unusual problem with you, and we shall see how it may be dispersed in our country air. There are so many remedies for unhappiness, and I intend to make it my business to find you one.

Respectfully,
Yours,
Estelle.

PS Kindly do not refer to me as '*marquésa*'. It implies that I am the property of the *marqués*, which I am not. I am a free star, which you should be. Your Queen's birthday should *not* be your concern. Can she not blow out her own candles?

E.

93 Avenida de Cervantes
Madrid

April 4th

Dear Janice,

This morning it rained. A cloudburst. The Gran Via was awash. So was I. I'd gone out to buy a calendar. A calendar in April?, you ask. I'll tell you why.

It's been a major decision day. After Piers had slipped out quiet as a mouse I realised that the real strain of all this was the not knowing, never knowing: did I have a marriage or not? Who/what was I? Where was I going? I closed my eyes and tried to conjure up all the people of iron resolution who might be an example to me – might show me the way. But I could only think of figures like Moses, Genghis Khan, Julius Caesar, Joan of Arc, General Schwarzkopf, and it didn't seem to me that any of them had a lot to offer me in the way of advice on marriage. Then another face appeared before me – Napoleon. He's my man, I thought. Napoleon. One hundred days – that was the length of his last campaign. So, that's the length of time I'll give myself to sort this thing out one way or the other. In that time I shall do everything in my power to bring Piers and me together. If I win, battle honours all round, though it may of course end in my Waterloo, in which case I shall gracefully draw a curtain across sixteen years of my life. (To think, Janice, I was married at twenty – the same age tweetie-pie is now. I wonder if Piers sees her as Ruth Reborn. Maybe he feels once was quite enough. How very sad.)

One hundred days – where would that take me? I've never been one for diaries: far too incriminating. That was why I went out to buy a calendar. There wasn't a great deal of choice at this time of the year. Besides, I was already drenched. I seized the nearest and largest, thrust some pesetas at the man, hastily rolled the thing up and scuttled home.

And there it is now, hanging on my bedroom wall. I've ringed the date when I shall either have a husband or not. One hundred days takes me to July 13th, which happens to be Friday the 13th, a trick of fate I could have done without. And not only that. The calendar when I unrolled it turned out to be a splendid advertisement for sun-tan lotion. Each month displays a nubile creature enjoying the sun in a startling landscape. Bugger it, I thought. Well, too late; I wasn't going to get drenched a second time. So I shall imagine each of these maidens to be her, since I'm determined never to meet the real one. April's girl is wandering among mountain-flowers with the Jungfrau in the background like a naked version of *The Sound of Music*. Maybe if I stick enough pins in her they'll deflate tweetie-pie's boobs, or perhaps she can be encouraged to tumble off a rocky ledge like the embassy's No 2, preferably without my Piers.

Suddenly I realised I was really no good at this at all. My Humpty Dumpty marriage had taken a great fall and I didn't know what to do. I'm used to being the cause of jealousy, not its victim. I'd been handed the wrong script without a clue how to play it.

What I needed was – HELP. Definitely. No more DIY marriage guidance. This was a job for the professionals. I decided to take a leaf out of grandmother Rosenthal's book. She used to say 'Always get the best. Beg them. Bribe them. Cajole them. Fuck them. Even pay them if you have to. But get the best.' Well, fortunately one of the very best in the present circumstances happens to be my sister-in-law Suzanne: you don't know her and mightn't want to (neither do I much), but she's a shit-hot sex-therapist – a self-appointed friend to all the fucked-up world. She lives in Bristol and writes books with clever titles like *Roles and Rules* – *The Guardian* loves them. She's got a radio phone-in, agony pages in the women's mags, and you get the impression no one could possibly get it right in bed without asking her first. For kicks she also runs Encounter Groups in which people are encouraged to insult and scream at each other. I went once with an old friend out of curiosity and called him a fucking shit, which he wasn't though it seemed to fit the mood of the evening, and he's never spoken to me since. So it's not truth I'm after, but weapons. Suzanne has plenty of these. She's adept at telling wives what they should be doing with their errant husbands. The respect she commands – and the fees – suggests it works. Certainly my brother is a faithful admirer – toes firmly on the line or they'd get chopped off along with other things. (I call him the Encounter Groupie.)

Suzanne answered the phone as if it was a starting pistol, and suddenly I panicked: I couldn't think what to say. 'You aren't in the middle of an encounter, are you?' I asked stupidly. As if she would be at nine in the morning. Suzanne obviously thought I meant 'Are you screwing?', and spluttered 'No, certainly not.' 'I didn't mean that,' I said, making it worse. 'Mean what?' she asked.

It was not a great beginning. Then I just dived through the barbed wire and told her what had happened. She lobbed it straight back at me. No commiserations: just 'Do you care?' 'Of course I bloody well care,' I shouted. Christ, I thought, this is becoming like an Encounter Group already. 'That's good', she said. Her voice was as cool as steel. 'You have an open marriage, you've often said. It's not easy to tell whether it's still open, or blown away. Your . . . er . . . revels would destroy most relationships, wouldn't they?' *This* is extremely painful, I told myself. I am being skinned. 'But my marriage isn't "most relationships",' I said bravely. 'Nor is Piers "most men."' A pause; then that cool voice again: 'Perhaps'. It was a 'perhaps' that meant 'rubbish'. 'Suzanne, our rules have been different,' I went on defiantly. 'But they've worked. And now he's broken them.'

I blundered on for quite a while – poured it all out. By the end I was screaming. Then she came back at me with the same quiet, deadly voice. 'If you're hurt and angry – tell him. If you care – let him see it. If he really loves her it may be too late. But what is Piers now? Forty. And she's twenty, you say. So, perhaps it's a youth game – many of them do try it – try to recapture something easier, more innocent, more pliant. He probably thinks she's a virgin: they all do. You may even find he doesn't really believe the whole thing himself. If that's the case, give him the excuse of your own pain and he may be glad to give it up.'

I started to cry. Perhaps she meant me to. Even on the phone I could feel the practised hand passing me the

Kleenex. Anyway she suddenly dropped her Amazon role and began to give me very calm, practical advice. I must sit him down, she said; make him understand exactly what I'm feeling, what he's done to me. I'm absolutely not to start saying it's partly my own fault – not enough attention to our marriage, and all that stuff. Let him have it straight. He's hurt me terribly: it's his responsibility, and up to him to put it right. Sock it to him.

In a nutshell those were the instructions of Encounter Gruppenführer (and an extremely expensive phone-call for Piers to pay: probably as much as he spends on dinner for tweetie-pie).

All right, I thought. I'll give it a go.

Now, the One Hundred Days is going to begin with an account of my efforts to put into practice the advice of Encounter Gruppenführer Suzanne, sister-in-law and professional sex-therapist.

Marital Repairs Service Report No 1

Janice, the God of Love possesses a distorted sense of humour. And maybe it's his sense of humour that enables us to endure the tricks he plays.

That evening I waited for Piers to come back from the embassy, rehearsing over and over again what I would say, what Gruppenführer had told me – 'Make him understand exactly what you're feeling, what he's done to you, how terribly he's hurt you. Don't start saying it's partly your own fault – it isn't. Let him have it straight. Sock it to him.'

I rehearsed and rehearsed. I walked up and down the

flat delivering heartrending speeches to the mirror, the pictures, the street outside, and occasionally to the sun-tan calendar when I needed to stoke my fires. I became amazingly eloquent, wonderfully lucid. My arguments were unanswerable. It was a superb performance, and I was proud of myself: I walked tall. I was going to greet him calmly, sit him down in a civilised fashion, and then one by one present him with my arguments – present him with my very soul – just as Suzanne said. I would make sure he listened – really listened; make sure he really understood, that he knew what deep psychic pain he was causing me – I who had always loved him deep down and trusted him implicitly when it came to the sanctity of our life together. And how he had broken that sacred trust: how could he? Oh yes, here I was, baring my heart to him, showing him how sorely that heart was bleeding. No stiff upper lip from Ruth Conway: I was going to let him have it straight, tell him just what he'd done to me; really sock it to him.

And when Piers came through the door that's exactly what I did. I said 'You fucking shit' and thumped him.

My knuckles are still extremely painful, but my goodness he did go down. It felt absolutely wonderful. Glorious release of tension – like the best of orgasms. And where did I get the strength? Unfortunately he struck his head on the radiator as he fell, and I thought I'd killed him. I panicked and immediately forgave him everything posthumously with all my heart, until he opened one eye and said 'Jesus, did you have to do that?'; whereupon I became furious again and shouted, 'Yes I did, you bloody bastard.'

He *was* bloody too. He left the apartment next morning with a couple of sticking plasters across his bald patch. He looked like a hot and very cross bun.

I'm afraid I wasn't made for sweet reason. I'm all high impulse or low cunning. And I certainly don't know where to turn for help next: I'll lick my wounds (while Piers licks his) and try to come up with another answer. I hope I'm not already on the road to Waterloo.

Anyway, I've temporarily abandoned Napoleonic strategy and reverted to foolish plots to discomfort Piers. They won't solve anything, but it may give me some satisfaction: a bit like going to bed with an utter shit – you can't stop in the middle because it feels too nice, but afterwards you wish you hadn't done it.

So, let me now present to you the case of the disappearing contemporary British sculpture.

Apparently there's an exhibition of the stuff opening this week. It seems the Brits have had to put up with a load of Spanish ironwork, and this is the *quid pro quo.* Piers hasn't been able to wriggle out of being *el padrino.* He has to open the thing with one of those speeches about hands across the ocean and the cross-fertilisation of cultures. He hates modern art with a passion, never having got much further than 450 BC. I on the other hand enjoy it because it's irreverent. The weirder the better. In embassy circles this is well known. Anybody who knows about anything modern in embassy circles is marked for life: they look at you amazed as if you've been badly brought up, which of course I have. Anyway, the word has got round. Xavier (the Interior Minister, remember?) rang me two days ago to explain that his government wished to make a gesture of good will and present a 'living work' (whatever that means) to our embassy, and please would I agree to choose it?

Today therefore I rang Xavier and arranged for a 'preview'. The show is in some agricultural hall on the edge of town. With the sculpture installed it looks even more like an agricultural hall. To my delight the man Xavier asked to take me round was Esteban, which made the place seem almost glamorous. He was looking gorgeous as usual – and incidentally invited me to a fund-raising lunch next week.

I'm not sure what Madrid will make of Britain's young Michelangelos. I was more concerned with what Piers might make of them. The centrepiece was a huge work by an awfully famous artist you undoubtedly know better than I do – Harrison Trench – the man who makes sculptures commemorating his journeys, usually miserably uncomfortable journeys to various godforsaken deserts: I should prefer to forget them, not commemorate them. However, this particular *magnum opus* I liked because I didn't understand it – which I always find helps with art. It was a vast pile of stones arranged as a sort of pyramid and entitled poetically '1549 stones'. Well, that's interesting, I thought: there must be a profound significance in it not being '1550 stones'. Some flunky pressed a catalogue on me – in English, which will help the Spaniards tremendously. 'The basis of Harrison Trench's work,' I read, 'is an intuition of the oneness of nature.' That's it, I decided. Just what Piers needs. 1549 stones to inform him of the essential oneness of nature in case he's forgotten, shaped like a pyramid to remind him of the closeness of death should he embrace the oneness of nature too bloody passionately.

I expressed misgivings about removing the centrepiece of so prestigious an exhibition before it even opened. But Esteban was undeterred. Being in commerce himself, he said, he would have no trouble replacing it with 1549 stones of an identical kind. Hence it seems that His Acting-Excellency Piers Conway will be able to contemplate the oneness of nature no later than Friday.

So, what with a wound in his head, pornography and paedophilia in his 'In' tray and a monstrous pyramid in the embassy courtyard, the diplomatic ladder of our Chargé d'Affaires may soon have some greasy rungs. I wonder if Estelle would approve. I shall phone and tell her.

The wonderful Estelle, I have to say, is a beacon of light in my darkness, partly for having no idea at all what my marriage problem is about. I might as well talk to her in Swahili. Her letters are a litany of the most engaging noncomprehension. I must collect them – perhaps include them in *Alas in Wonderland* ('copyright the Marquésa de Trujillo y Toledo'). I must go and visit her, taking care to avoid the mornings when she's the Duchess of Windsor and the afternoons when she's asleep or something. I also think I want to find out more about Esteban – with whom I have lunch next week. I trust it's not only funds he's capable of raising.

I joke. I always joke when I'm low. I sometimes wonder, if/when this ever ends, whether there could be anything of my marriage left. You've finally torn up yours: all those years when I urged you to do so I never believed it could be so painful a thing to contemplate. You tear up roots. You tear up a life. You tear yourself in half.

Please go on cheering me up with events in River Mews. And good luck with the Creepy Crawlies. Have you considered that Attila's supergun might be the one Saddam Hussein ordered?

You know, if money gets tight you can always move into our flat and rent out the house. I'm quite serious. You're my dearest friend. Piers is my dearest enemy.

With much love,

Ruth.

British Embassy
Madrid

April 7th

Dear Harry,

You are right that Heads of Mission quite often lose their marbles, but a little hasty in assuming I have lost mine.

Oriental religions are *not* 'a load of mystical mumbo-jumbo,' as you so stylishly put it. I quoted Hinduism to you on the telephone merely to illustrate that not all amorous delights are physical (I might as easily have quoted Dante and Beatrice), not to prove to you that, in your words, I am a 'hypocritical old sentimentalist'. If you were not one of my oldest friends I might take offence: as it is I shall merely point out that you can be an insensitive ass. The truth is, I am neither Romeo nor Don Juan.

Angelica is scarcely half my age. She is entirely inexperienced. A physical relationship would hasten us both along a path of destruction. I am convinced of this. She is the most beautiful of creatures. I love her. She is, as I have told you, an angel with dew on her wings. But we shall not be lovers: I am certain.

Unfortunately it seems impossible to convey this to Ruth. She will hear nothing. The other evening I returned home intent on spelling out the precise nature of my relationship with Angelica. But before I could utter a word she struck me a blow that would have felled Mike Tyson. I bear the scars.

So of course does she. I admit I am deeply troubled: guilt and helplessness ride in tandem. The prospect of a world without Ruth is a nightmare. If I lose her I lose myself. Yet Angelica has touched something in me that was dying, and has given it life. The desert flowers. When I set eyes on her I feel joy. Harry, I like to think of myself as a good man, and know for certain I am not. I am 'in thrall' – not a state I recommend. Lovers are dangerous clowns.

You may consider an ambassador's private office to be an unusual place in which to write about such things. Not so, I assure you. When the office of our late-lamented No 2 was cleared following her demise, one drawer of her locked desk was found to be stuffed with memos from my distinguished predecessor. To describe these as '*billets doux*' would do poor justice to Sir Randolph's powers of imagery, particularly as applied to the female anatomy. Sadly we do not have her replies: doubtless she preferred deeds to words, and – alas – perished in the deed.

Conway's Law is proving less reliable than I hoped. They are finding me things to do. The new Labour Deputy Foreign Minister is due out here about the time of the Queen's Birthday to discuss among other things the future of the Rock. We can only hope he doesn't think it's something you eat, with 'Gibraltar' written right through it. At least, unlike Reagan, he may be relied upon to know which country he's in.

So, time is no longer on my hands. Dear Angelica clearly believes it is – bless her. She has just had delivered for me a mountain of books on philosophy and photography from the British Council library. I wonder why. She is entirely adorable. I can't imagine Ruth ever troubling to do such a thing.

Talking of mountains, I have just arranged for a crude pile of rocks to be removed from the forecourt where they were obstructing the cars. The truck-driver insisted they were intended for the embassy, but I pointed out there were no building works here at present, and refused to sign for them. There is a multi-storey car park under construction across the road and I directed him there. In retrospect perhaps I should have kept the rocks as a barricade against the Deputy Foreign Minister. Too late now.

I'm delighted your private life improves. But if she is a senator's wife how long will it remain private? How long does your private life *ever* remain private?

Very best wishes, insensitive though you may be.

Yours,

Piers.

93 Avenida de Cervantes
Madrid

April 10th

Dear Janice,

The fund-raising lunch was a triumph. I had to give an impromptu speech before an audience of thirty, would you believe? Somewhat at a loss, I spoke about the Victoria and Albert Museum and its traditional links with trade and industry. This seemed to go down well. Esteban had rustled up a bunch of cigar-smoking desperadoes from the commercial milieu who must have been eyeing some backhanders in all this, though I can't imagine what an exhibition of conquistadors' loot can possibly offer them. They certainly eyed me: I received four propositions over coffee and brandy. No Spanish *hidalgo*, I've learnt, invites you to inspect his etchings: it's 'My wife and I would be honoured to receive you at our *castillo*', and you know perfectly well that his wife will have been called away at the last minute to nurse a sick relative. This particular gentleman didn't even have a wife. 'Dead for years,' Esteban whispered to me. 'It's generally believed he killed her.'

Well, I was learning a few things. Esteban retained a watchful look throughout: I think he wanted to make sure that if Her Excellency chose to stray it would be in the direction of his own *castillo* – or *hacienda* in his case: he has one not far from Estelle, his aunt, he made a point of telling me. 'Very peaceful.'

I bet.

But all very good for the libido. And it helped put tweetie-pie out of my mind for a few hours. I can do with that.

And it also gave me another battle-plan for despatching the little bitch. There was only one woman at the lunch – wife of the Israeli Ambassador. I took to her, and she to me. I had to sidestep the question of whether I was a practising Jew, explaining we'd only just arrived in Spain and hadn't yet had a chance to locate the local synagogue. She offered to introduce me to the rabbi, who also officiates at their embassy. I accepted.

What was strange, Janice, was that I wanted to accept. Perhaps we return to spiritual homes when we need comfort. I remembered all the mutterings and chantings of my childhood, and felt quite nostalgic. Nothing, I thought, could be more different from Gruppenführer – no post-Freudian insights, just the wisdom of ancient traditions. After my fiasco of 'Encountering' Piers, a rabbi seemed exactly the person I needed to talk to.

So I did – this afternoon. He was agelessly bearded and avuncular, and held my hands. I couldn't help it – I cried gently. We talked for two hours, it must have been. There was quite a lot of 'a good Jewish wife needs to be . . .', and all that stuff. And even this was comforting. Then, having got that off his chest, he became wonderfully clear-headed and rather cunning. A wife, he assured me with huge authority, has a great advantage over a man's mistress – she *knows* him. Knows his needs, his foibles, his weaknesses: 'and having a young lover is most uncomfortable, you should remember.'

I must say, I'd never imagined discomfort might be what Piers experienced when he lay in bed with his mistress, but the rabbi – he was called Isaac naturally – promised me it was so (how did he know?). He explained that while adultery might bring fleeting joys, it also induced in the adulterer a longing for the more sober and familiar pleasures he'd left behind. 'A lover needs always to be at his best. This imposes a terrible strain; whereas a husband may gladly admit to being sometimes tired, or bad-tempered, or dull.'

The vision of Piers longing to be bad-tempered and dull with me while tearing tweetie-pie's clothes off struck me as hilariously unlikely. And yet there was something in the rabbi's manner which bred confidence. Or perhaps I just wanted to believe it. He talked soothingly about how marriage was rooted in the small and trusted things of daily life – its routines, its certainties, habits, shared memories. These were what Piers would be missing – he was quite sure of it. (Shared memories! Oh God, I thought, a handful of the wrong ones might just drive Piers away for ever.)

Suddenly Isaac looked at me sharply. '*Are* you a good wife?' The eyebrows loomed over me like thunderclouds. 'Do you care for Piers? Do you cherish him?' Oh Janice, horrific scenes of Conway marital bliss rose before my eyes. Me dragging Piers off to the opera when he said he was ill, accusing him of being a hypochondriac wimp: then he collapsed with pneumonia. Or trying to dry his socks in the oven – I'd promised he could have them to wear for a meeting. They were nylon and burned to little crispy bits. And the *bouillabaisse* I once served him: he swore the fish's eye winked at him. Isaac, I suspected, knew all too well about my skills as a wife. The eyebrows gathered like the wrath of Jove. 'Sometimes,' I ventured feebly, 'I like to cook for him.' No storm broke. The rabbi's face relaxed into kindliness: perhaps I'd said the right thing at last. 'In which case,' he answered, 'may I suggest you display your skills? Create an atmosphere of warmth, of family. Do not always be angry because he has transgressed. Your strength is that you are the wife he loves. Use that strength. But use it mildly,' he went on with a wise smile. 'Invite friends in. Let your husband see how others value you. He will see what he risks losing.'

He then offered to lend me a kosher cook-book his own wife often used. I thanked him profusely before declining his offer on the grounds that my shelves were positively crammed with cook-books (actually I have two – *Microwave cooking made easy*, and Josceline Dimbleby's *Marvellous Meals with Mince*). I didn't dare confess that Piers was a gentile with a terrible passion for suckling pig: and then the thought came to me – Spain is the land of the suckling pig, and next week is Piers' birthday! Maybe here was the chance to prove myself the perfect non-Jewish wife. Before my eyes rose a scene of gastronomic splendour: no colour supplement could do justice to it – eat your heart out Delia Smith. 'Oh Ruth, forgive me,' I could hear Piers whisper as the last guest departed with an admiring kiss of my hand. 'Never again will I transgress.'

Well, something like that.

Janice, the idea has seriously got to me. On my way back from seeing Isaac I bought a book on Spanish cooking in the Gran Via. Lots of pictures; ingredients and quantities clearly stated; instructions straightforward. I'm now going to plan the intimate dinner party of the year; and if Piers still prefers tweetie-pie's 'spag bol' after that I'll put the stuffing where it belongs.

Next thing – the menu. 'Keep it simple' is always a good rule, isn't it?, though personally I've never had much choice. I have the cook-book in front of me. To begin with – *gazpacho* sounds a good idea: it's only cold soup, after all; Piers is always complaining my soup is cold anyway. No problem there. To be followed by . . . something artistic with fresh prawns I like the idea of – I'll get myself to the fish-market first thing in the morning. Then the suckling pig – my *pièce de résistance*. Our new maid Teresa is forever bringing me delicious tit-bits from her mother's kitchen: she will be my guardian angel. Besides, we have a rotisserie oven in the flat: I shall baptise it gloriously. The dessert – well, I'll brood over that.

So, screw fund-raising for the next few days. And thank you, Rabbi Isaac, for your wise counsel. I should like to ask you to join the feast, but roast suckling pig may not be your favourite nosh. Who, then, shall I invite? Tom Brand if he's arrived in Madrid: he'll be gallantly on my side. The Second Secretary and his wife who's elegant but has no tits, so no competition there. And perhaps one other couple. Dare I ask the Minister of Finance, who will be guaranteed to flirt with me? His wife is half-blind and won't notice. I trust Piers will.

And I shall dress to kill.

More later. Wish me luck. My love as ever, and a big kiss for my genius of a godson,

Ruth.

1 River Mews

April 16th

My dear Ruth,

You seem in amazingly good spirits. I admire your *chutzpah* (isn't that what Rabbi Isaac would call it?). I trust Piers will admire your suckling pig as much.

Do you really believe I'm better at living alone than you are at being married? It doesn't always feel like that. Once Piers has given up hunting for his lost youth you at least will have something to return to – I'm certain of that: I know Piers, he has a naive romantic streak. Whereas for me the future seems an empty land. Sometimes I love the freedom of it – I can wander where I will. At other times, alone and unemployed, I grow frightened – the best years slipping away, marriage a disaster, my looks living on borrowed time. And then I look at Tom Brand – he's grey, he's lined, he's almost twenty years older than I am – and it simply *doesn't matter.* Heads still turn when he enters a restaurant, the bastard. They won't for me when I'm 55, except to say charitably, 'She must have been quite good-looking once.' It makes me understand why security matters so much more for women than it does for men. We live under the tyranny of mirrors.

Those are the bad days. On good mornings I look at myself and say 'Janice, you could have anyone you want. Anyone.' But who *do* I want? Tinker. Tailor. Soldier. Sailor . . . Part of me has always rather fancied the Thief – provided I'm the one who gets stolen. By Tom? That question again. He certainly persists. Well, *you* know all about that.

Yes, I'm broke. The Indian polo-player's nonsense for his swimming-pool has fallen through. No reason given. Bill is despondent: 'Usual playboy behaviour – the rule of iron whim.' So I've gone out to work – yes, I serve in the local deli – about which more later. The offer of your flat was incredibly kind. I'm deeply touched. But there's a lonely pride in me, Ruth: I want to beat this on my own. I'm going to live by my own work, however menial that work may have to be.

Now, let me bring you good cheer as you asked. Spring has come to River Mews; so it's the battle of the front gardens once again. Competition is a bit lack-lustre this year (perhaps aided by the post-suicidal gloom of Ah-man-dah, Harry's ex-lay down the road). Even so, now I'm a veteran of two springs here I do notice how front gardens undergo changes to match the personality of their owners. Dr. Angus and his frowning wife at No 4 never change, of course: the same his'n hers Ford Escorts keep their distance on the tarmac. A crocus struggled into bloom last week: this week duly crushed – rather like his one little uprising with me.

Roger the historian's solitary tree at No 5 has been severely lopped in my absence – again I fear something to do with me. At No 6 the Creepy Crawleys have laid an immaculate lawn – a displacement activity, I would think, not having laid each other for years. 'We have separate rooms,' Mrs Creepy volunteered last week, as though to assure me she'd long ago put away childish things. She'd called in uninvited for tea ('Camomile if you have it, Mrs Blakemore'; she calls me that to make me sound respectable). Her fear for me is that I'm in mortal danger

– a woman alone, vulnerable to predators, weak like all our sex (except her, naturally). I see her peering at Tom Brand when he arrives laden with booze and flowers. 'I feel sure that man must be married. Is he?' she asked yesterday. I smiled my sweetest. 'Oh yes,' I said. 'Five times.'

On down the gardens swiftly. No 7 – Bill and Nina: no recession in the architecture trade can blight that abandoned splash of wild-flowers, though I do notice Nina has added a fine crop of snakes'-heads, which makes me wonder what Bill told her, and whether she believed him. Dear virtuous Bill, the only one who said 'No' to me. Nina certainly plays tennis more aggressively than before. She's even invested in one of those sportswomen's bras – you know, the sort with a halter round the neck to steady the bounce. A winch more than a bra.

At No 8 Louisa's life-size carving of a figure raising arms to heaven ('Woman adjusting shower-curtain' – everyone now calls it that) has been attacked by woodworm, though Kevin's convinced it's death-watch beetle spread from Louisa. She's also discovered a new Himalayan sect with a branch in Uxbridge, which keeps her busy. It keeps Ambrose busy too. He drives her there twice a week in penance for having painted me nude. Sackcloth to add to the ashes of my portrait.

Lottie's front garden at No 9 used to be as empty as her life. Now, with Maurice in Gulag Macclesfield and Attila in active residence, it's become the overspill of her Renaissance – bottles, beer-cans, take-away pizza cartons, all bursting out of dustbins along with more intimate evidence and strewn for public inspection by the local cats. The Creepy Crawleys tut-tut as they go by, but

Lottie greets them with a beatific smile. She wanders in an erotic dream of Barbados and black skin. And to think that Maurice still imagines her lodger to hail from an ancient Highlands family – Bannockburn Macgregor Esquire.

On to No 10. Ah-man-dah – she of the homeopathic overdose. You may remember her celebrated oriental tree protected by a sack in winter and an alarm system linked directly to the local police-station. It died. Ah-man-dah has come to resemble the sack.

I believe I'm even nastier about her than Kevin. But then I have reason to be.

I've saved Kevin to the last for your entertainment. Not his front garden, which was never more than a bimbo park. No – his wife. I told you she'd come back, to Kevin's horror. Well, I'd just stepped out of the shower on Sunday morning when somebody began to play a triumphant tune on the front doorbell. I wrapped a towel round me and peered cautiously outside. Kevin was hopping up and down like a child. 'I done it,' he announced. 'I done it. Got rid of 'er.' 'How?' I asked, my hair dripping on the doorstep. 'Simple,' he said. 'Actually not simple at all. Bloody 'ard work. Two months I've 'ad of lovin' care 'n attention, fulfillin' a man's needs and all that. Right, I decided, I know what my needs are, and cos of 'er I've been deprived of 'em, 'aven't I? So what did I do? I fucked 'er day an' night, didn't I? Like the Grand Ole Duke of York I was - when 'e was up 'e was up. Finally she raised the white flag: said she was too old for that sort a thing. And back to the country licketty-split she went . . . Janice darlin', I done it.'

With that he lifted me off the ground and whirled me round and round, my hair whizzing about like a garden sprinkler, towel just about managing to hang on to some of the vital bits. Unfortunately the Creepy Crawleys chose that moment to stroll by on their way to Holy Communion. I don't imagine she'll be calling in for camomile tea again. I may even be outlawed from her prayers.

So that is spring fever in River Mews.

And now my job – I promised to tell you. A very superior local deli had a notice on the door asking for a female assistant. I'm a regular customer. The owner's Chinese – Ching, he's called – always addresses me as 'madam', bows a little, and insists on carrying my stuff to the car.

Ching's face when I said I'd like the job destroyed all myths of the inscrutable oriental. At first he seemed to think I was taking the piss – that unfathomable British sense of humour again. Then he became merely perplexed: 'Oh no, madam. Not for you. You a lady, not shop-girl.' 'I'm happy to be a shop-girl,' I said. 'I need a job. Reasonable hours. No distance from my home. And I like it here. Hams. Cheeses. Pasta. Quiches. Better than an office any day. Besides, I like *you*.' That threw him completely. He looked a beaten man. 'When shall I start, then?' I asked. 'Monday,' he squeaked miserably. 'You're on,' I said, and shook his hand. It was shaking already.

That was last Monday. And I enormously enjoy it. Better than painting pseudo-Hockneys for Indian polo-players. Keeps body and soul apart. I can survive on what he pays me. And I learn a lot.

The first thing I learnt, let me tell you, was the absolute necessity of wearing a bra. You may wonder why? Well, Ching is well known for his coffee. People come from miles around. The coffee-beans are in sacks on the floor. I have to bend over with one of those shovel things. This is not a posture for keeping secrets. One man came in three times on that first day: he could have opened a canteen with all the coffee he bought. The Rev. Hope developed a stammer and wiped his eyes. My bank manager's epiglottis went into spasm. And Kevin, who'd promised me a visit, announced to a crowded shop, 'Not quite enough there for Mountain Blend, darlin', I'm afraid.' When I tried to hold my jumper in with one hand I managed to spill the coffee-beans all over the floor; and picking them up of course made it worse.

Sales, I have to say, rocketted. Ching, who never looks at me anyway, puts it all down to my electric personality, and gave me a bonus.

But I do now own a bra. If you need help with the Queen's Birthday bash, I promise to wear it, though it does make me a shape I don't recognise.

Tom insists he's going to cook me his famous Moroccan *tajine* as soon as he's back from serenading you in Madrid. I may even surprise him by accepting. I'm assuming it will be low music and low intentions. I might just succumb. Five months! – I'm beginning to feel decidedly horny, and Tom's the best thing on offer at present – in fact the only thing on offer apart from Kevin. Why is it always grey-haired old lechers who fancy me?

Esteban sounds dreadful.

Clive has been asked to give a recital at the Wigmore

Hall. Have I bred the new Menuhin? He's much more excited about the new cricket season, especially since Attila has promised to take him into the pavilion at the Oval for Surrey's opening match. 'Stuff Mozart,' says Clive. Can a genius be a philistine? It would seem so.

With love as always, and good luck with the pig (I mean the suckling one, not Piers),

Janice (Shop assistant, Ching's Deli).

Palacio Pizarro
Trujillo

April 16th

Dear Ruth Conway,

I believe I do see your problem, after giving it much thought.

It comes from the foolish Anglo-Saxon habit of viewing all matters of the heart back to front (we French call it '*le vice anglais*'). I suggest you see what has happened to you as a French woman would. You are in the most excellent situation. You have a husband who swears he loves you, but has now taken a young mistress. So – you may now politely insist he leave, which permits you to be free, well-loved and well provided-for. How is it the American song goes? – 'Could you ask for anything more?'

True, it was not precisely like that in the case of Xavier and myself. It was I who took the young lover – or maybe several, I forget now. But he was intensely relieved, the dear man. Our friendship blossomed most agreeably: there were no longer pressures of unwanted duty. Surely after so many years (sixteen, is it?) there cannot be anything new for the two of you to experience together, and you say you are unable to bear children. Then, why not enjoy the wide world? You are still young. By my age the world narrows, but I have my memories. I have lived a rich life.

Do I really need to tell you why a man may sometimes prefer a younger woman? It is nothing to do with any of the things you suggest. It is simply a question of *mamelons* – the English word eludes me for the moment. No, I remember: it is *nipples*. A young woman's nipples point upwards; an older woman's downwards. That is all. I do not grasp the significance, and remain neutral since mine have always pointed straight ahead. But I know that men tend to enjoy trivial novelties. Perhaps we all do, and tire of them as quickly. If it continues to trouble you, I suggest you place your trust in the law of gravity: it will soon prevail. Time solves all such problems.

When are you coming to visit me? Xavier tells me you are already a bright star in Madrid. I detest the place. Here the countryside is fresh with young corn as far as Portugal. How reassuring that a national boundary should also be one's own.

I have no advice to offer on kitchen matters. Why does your cook not know?

Yours,

Estelle.

93 Avenida de Cervantes
Madrid

April 19th

Dear Janice,

Fifteen days ticked off on the calendar. Eighty-five to go, and I shall now tell you about Piers' birthday dinner.

Marital Repairs Service Report No 2

It was a warm spring morning. I made out my shopping-list under the surveillance of Teresa our maid, who also directed me to the best shops and market stalls. I needed a special journey for the suckling pig which was somewhat larger than I expected, even though we were to be eight for dinner – the eighth being an unsuitable lady I found for Tom Brand who'd announced his arrival the evening before.

Excitement and self-confidence mounted as the day progressed. Teresa was a pillar of strength, chopping, marinading, stirring, sloshing wine everywhere. But I was determined this was to be my show, not hers; so once she'd laid the table I dismissed her and set to work, my new Spanish cook-book open before me. At last after sixteen years I began to appreciate the joys of being a housewife. This, I thought, is clearly what has been wrong with my marriage: I shall now attend to it. Thank you Rabbi Isaac. Tom agreed to advise on wine, and sweetly went out and bought it. Then, with oceans of time on my hands I took a bath, washed my hair, and dressed at my leisure.

You have to picture me. Black velvet dress, hem three inches above the knee, figure-hugging but not skin-tight, no sleeves, cut across the top with two slender supporting straps. Black lycra tights. Black suede shoes with three-inch heels. Butler and Wilson gee-gaw dangly earrings – imitation antique gold with diamonds, plus bracelet with cupids and hearts (Piers gave it to me in London last year). Perfume – Jean Patou's 'Joy', v. expensive, as you know.

I gazed up at the girl in the sun-tan calendar. 'You got nothing on me, kid,' I said. (True, she had nothing on anyway.)

There I was – ready. The evening lay before me. The guests were to be as I bravely predicted. A small party. The Second Secretary who is boyish and literary, and his wife who is boyish and illiterate. The Minister of Finance accepted gladly to my great surprise: my fund-raising activities are obviously getting round, or my reputation is. He's cross-eyed – one eye stays put, the other goes walkabout – rather like a dog on one of those extendable leads, occasionally getting yanked back for cocking its leg in unsuitable places. His wife is myopic, perhaps from half a lifetime of turning a blind eye on her husband's wanderings. For all that, they're good company. Then Tom Brand, who promised to be ultra-suave: he speaks Spanish, so he claims (I suspect of the '*Viva España*' variety). The lady I provided for him is no Janice – I took care of that: a teacher at the American School – very WASP, with no sting, but a large nose and a small moustache.

Finally, of course, Piers. It was very hard to tell if he felt uncomfortable. I hoped not. For the last week I haven't mentioned tweetie-pie at all – as if she didn't exist. The last time was when he came into my bedroom all hot and bothered searching for his cufflinks. 'What you need is handcuffs,' I suggested. I saw the surprise on his face as he caught sight of the sun-tan calendar. 'Does she look like that, your girl?' I asked. He fluffed, then muttered, 'How would I know?' I laughed.

That was the last time. How would he know? Bloody cheek. He knows every curve and dimple on her body, the louse.

The guests began to arrive around nine: this is Spain, remember. There were flowers for me, little wrapped gifts for Piers who was embarrassed, and much chatter over drinks. Tom did the honours and generally behaved as though he was the host. Piers behaved as though he'd come to the wrong house (he probably felt he had). I noticed that the Finance Minister's left eye enjoyed the American teacher less than his right eye enjoyed me. The Second Secretary talked about South American novels, which brought Piers out of his shell because he's a devotee of Marquez. I scored heavily by pretending I'd read the entire works of Benito Peréz Galdós. 'Our Balzac,' exclaimed the Minister proudly. 'Only better,' I chipped in, implying that I'd read all Balzac too. And on that triumphant breeze I wafted into the kitchen, pursued by the Finance Minister's right eye.

The rest of the evening I prefer to summarise.

We started with the *gazpacho*. Cold soup – right! Well, it was certainly cold: I'd put it in the freezer to make sure. An hour would be about right, I thought. I was wrong. We had rather a delayed start while I unfroze it over the gas-stove. I think it boiled a bit at the edges, but I stirred the ice around to equalise it. It didn't taste at all bad to me, though Teresa had never told me I was supposed to skin the tomatoes before mixing them with the other exciting ingredients. So I'm afraid that in addition to the melting-icecap effect the tomato skins gave the impression of a shipwrecked cargo of red vests. The croutons weren't a great deal of help either. I gather they're meant to be fried crisp. Well, mine weren't. They clung to the red vests like disintegrating frog-spawn. The Second Secretary and his wife were politeness itself. The Minister seemed quite skilled at navigating this Sargasso Sea, and Tom could be heard bravely crunching down the last bits of ice-flow. But the American teacher was timid and stuck to the shallows. 'Delicious,' she said, leaving most of it. 'What is it?'

I awarded myself half-marks only for the *gazpacho* and was slightly cross with myself for the red vests. However, I *had* tried; and I confidently moved on to the garlic prawns. Now things took a distinct turn for the better. No mistakes at all. They're dead easy, aren't they? Teresa had shown me how to skin the prawns, breaking off their heads and little legs. Then I fried them in a mixture of oil and butter with lashings of chopped garlic, all served up in individual dishes with chopped parsley on the top.

They were a *succés fou.* Conversation returned. Piers began to look as though he was proud of me. Tom poured out lots of white Rioja. I poured perhaps a bit too much down myself, which loosened my tongue. There was only one bad moment, which I instantly regretted. The

Minister's wife was saying she'd rarely enjoyed prawns more, and had I thought of writing a sea-food cookbook?; to which I replied without thinking, 'Indeed I have: I'm going to call it *Prawnography*'. She looked mystified. Nobody else did. Tom tried not to double up. The Minister's right eye brightened. Piers lowered his head. I turned mine away – though I have to say I thought it was rather witty at the time.

This seemed the moment for my *pièce de résistance* – the suckling pig. I'd had one or two problems with this early on. Not major ones, but little irritants I could have done without on an occasion like this. For instance, Teresa told me I needed to soak the pig to get the blood out. Well, I forgot. Perhaps I was offended by the idea – depriving the poor creature of its lifeblood. Anyway, at worst it would mean the meat wasn't white, as it ought to be, but a less appealing reddish-pink; also that there might be quite a lot of red gravy flying around the rotisserie oven while it turned. I wasn't too happy about that. In fact I assumed this was what had happened when I began to smell burning. It wasn't. I opened the oven door to a jet of flame. One of the pig's ears was on fire. Not only that. I told you it was rather a large animal, and indeed I'd had some trouble getting it safely into the oven. I thought I'd managed it. Unfortunately, when I'd thrown enough water on the flames to extinguish them I realised one of the pig's trotters had got stuck, so that the rotisserie hadn't been able to turn properly. In fact I don't believe it had turned at all, judging by the look of it. There was this persistent clanking noise, with nothing happening.

I did the best I could. At least I knew the green

vegetables would be all right. I'd done them well in advance, and they were keeping warm in their water on the stove. And the rice was nice and smooth – I'd had to add a bit more liquid before the guests arrived to make sure it didn't dry out: rice has to be good and moist or it gets stuck in your teeth. There was also salad as a side-dish: the Spaniards like things strong, so I'd given it plenty of bite with some flakes of chilli, lots of malt vinegar and a good dash of tabasco (my idea, remembered from our Mexican days).

But the pig was tricky. The burnt ear had more or less disintegrated: the animal looked a bit funny with just one ear, but I knew no one would mind that. I wasn't so happy about the rest of it. Quite apart from the problem of getting it out of the oven, I could see that it wasn't exactly cooked evenly, I suppose because the rotisserie hadn't been able to turn. However, there was nothing I could do about it now, and I asked Tom to carve while I fetched the rice and veg out of the warm water.

Janice, this was the moment when I began to realise that Rabbi Isaac's advice was perhaps not for me. I wish I could draw a veil over the suckling pig (Oh Teresa, where were you?). One side, I'm afraid, was black as charcoal, the other entirely raw. There was some kind of compromise on the borderlands, but only the narrowest of strips. Tom did nobly, but one slither of part-raw part-charred pork on each plate was not the feast I'd planned; and even I thought the vegetables were a trifle damp. The water, what's more, mixed less than happily with the pig's blood, though the rice did mop it up a bit. After the first mouthful Piers tried to freshen his mouth with the salad, and only just made it to the bathroom before he threw up. Soon afterwards the other guests made it to the door before I remembered the sweet – or, to be truthful, before I remembered I'd entirely forgotten to make one. Tom stayed behind and comforted me. Then an awful silence hung over the place, along with an equally awful smell. After Tom had departed Piers emerged looking pale. 'Good night,' he said, '. . . and I'm sorry.' I said 'Happy birthday, my darling,' and burst into tears.

Resolution 1: To stay away from synagogues.
Resolution 2: To get in caterers for the Queen's Birthday.
Resolution 3: To go out with Tom tonight and get smashed.

I'll put this in the post first.
With much love,
Ruth.

British Embassy
Madrid

April 23rd

Dear Harry,

I remember as a child that birthdays invariably ended in tears. They still do.

My own last week was an ill-conceived affair. I had been looking forward to an evening alone with Ruth – a restorative evening, I hoped. What occurred was Restoration Comedy. Instead of a quiet dinner *à deux*, allowing me to get across to Ruth that my relationship with Angelica is platonic, a surprise dinner-party was arranged for my benefit. Several surprises, as it transpired. My least favourite of Ruth's courtiers turned up – Tom Brand, the tabloid hack. So did my own Second Secretary who I see every day and could have done without on this occasion; plus his imbecilic wife widely known (except apparently to Ruth) to be the tearful mistress (among many) of the Spanish Finance Minister, who was another of our party. His own wife is openly lesbian, partly living with a moustached lady from Wisconsin who (you may have guessed by now) was also present.

It was not a jolly evening. Nor was it improved by Ruth's determination to do the cooking herself – never a good idea. Fortunately the next day was Sunday, which gave me time to recover. I can't vouch for the others.

At least the Queen's Birthday bun-fight was spared Ruth's flame-thrower cuisine. I'd arranged for a marquee in the embassy garden, and did my best to host the visiting minister from the Foreign Office. I suppose – and you as a journalist would know – when one has been in opposition for twelve years one's perception of world affairs must lack a certain freshness; however, I had expected him to know that General Franco was dead. I may of course be doing him an injustice, and it was merely the bullish tone of his speech which gave the impression he was addressing a fascist regime. No doubt he had been preparing it for the past twelve years. Fortunately he spoke in English with such a fine Geordie accent that it was safe to assume no one understood a word he uttered.

Ruth, I have to say, was not of that view. After we had made the loyal toast to Her Majesty she jumped nobly – and rather publicly – to the defence of liberal values here in Spain, button-holing the confused junior minister. I was exceedingly proud of her up to the point when those liberal values began to go rather strongly to her head. My predecessor's excellent taste in wine may have contributed to this. In any case yesterday morning's papers made something of a meal of her remark that Gibraltar was only a bloody rock and the Spaniards were welcome to it provided they undertook to look after the monkeys. I'm afraid the press thought she was referring to the British population living in Gibraltar, and there were several inventive cartoons illustrating this point.

As you may imagine, all this kept me busy. The phone-call from No 10 was not unequivocally complimentary, though I managed to defuse matters by assuring the PM that my wife's remarks were intended to be purely ecological and given a quite erroneous political significance by uninvited Spanish journalists.

In short, Ruth does not change. As for Conway's Law, that has long ceased to be enforceable.

Thankfully the third birthday was not tearful. It was Angelica's. She admitted to it being only her twentieth: she had been shy, she said, of being a mere teenager when I met her. I found that touching. She is the loveliest of creatures: I am in heaven just gazing at her. I have made a promise to take her to Toledo for a weekend shortly: she is enamoured of El Greco, and indeed often reminds me of one of his Madonnas.

I'm not sure how to take your likening me to a 'puritanical Humbert Humbert'. As for Angelica being almost certainly a 'right little raver' if only I had the sense to see it: you know, there are women in the world who look for something other than a *membrum virile*, even if you take good care never to meet them.

I was perturbed on your behalf to hear who the senator is. I trust his wife is discretion itself or your Washington days are certainly numbered. Any further observations by Ruth on the future of the Rock, and so will mine be here.

Perhaps we shall both of us end up in Beirut – hostages to our own fate if not to the Hizbollah.

As ever,
Yours,
Piers.

16c Iffley Street
Hammersmith
London W6

April 25th

Dear Madam Excellency,

I had no idea what you've been going through, and to see you brought so low was a shock. I don't know whether our sweet/sad evening in Madrid helped. The wine seemed to, at least. You said being with someone you'd known almost as long as Piers was a comfort. That was touching. I may not be the man for you (and after fifteen years it's probably time I recognised that), but what we do have is friendship – a rarer thing than romance or sex, perhaps more durable.

Forgive me for being sentimental. I am.

The last thing you need now is a homily from me. Just let me know if there's anything at all I can do. Knee-jerk Piers? Write you anonymous lover-letters on House of Lords notepaper? Seduce the girl? Maybe just hop on a plane and take you out for another long late dinner? Of all my suggestions that would be the easiest to fix: the Spanish drug-running story is ongoing, and if that should fizzle out I know at least three top officials in Madrid who are diverting E.C. farm subsidies into Swiss bank accounts (the trouble is, they're also useful contacts).

I have one severe complaint to make. Your comments about the monkeys in Gibraltar pushed a story of mine off the front page. I trust Piers suffered. I thought he looked seedy at the Birthday bash. You on the other hand looked magnificent. Red matches the fire in you, and you certainly burnt up that little prat from the F.O. Did you know he was spotted cruising later that evening? I have two witnesses. You see, there's another story that could bring me to Madrid. The trouble is, my esteemed editor enjoys similar pastimes – for which I have considerably more than two witnesses. I'll keep that story for the day I'm fired.

For what it's worth, let me offer you a thought. Middle age hits men with fantasies – usually sexual. Depending on our nature we either agonise over them, or live them out. Piers, I would guess, is the agonising kind: all guilt and longings, no action. I know you'll think I'm wrong – but you wait. I bet the girl's a holy shrine, and his love for her is all incense and bruised knees. This insight may be crass, but it comes from a recognition of opposites. I once fell in love with someone even younger than Piers's girl. I remember all that virginal purity stuff. Not being an agoniser I married her after three weeks. The marriage lasted three months. It cost me a small house, a large car, and a smashed dream. With men like Piers it takes longer, but there may be less bomb-damage in the end.

Forgive me for being Doubting Thomas. But I am your friend – remember.

I called in to see Janice in her deli. In her case 'deli' is short for 'delicious'. She serves prosciutto as though it was a love-feast. I wish it was. I'm preparing her a Moroccan dinner on Tuesday. Only good lovers can be good cooks, I told her. She handed me the prosciutto with a delectable smile and said she was on a diet.

I wonder.

Don't let the priestly Piers get the better of you. You're worth ten of him. Come to think of it, so am I.

As always,

Tom.

LONDON W6 1100 HRS APRIL 28
CABLE DESPATCH TO: RUTH CONWAY 93
AVENIDA CERVANTES MADRID SPAIN
PRAWNOGRAPHY COOKBOOK BRILLIANT
IDEA HAVE INTERNATIONAL PUBLISHER
INTERESTED STOP MYSELF DOING
ILLUSTRATIONS PLUS RESEARCH HO HO IDEAS
PLENTIFUL MIND BOGGLES PLEASE CON-
TRIBUTE STOP LOVE CHEERFULLY JANICE

May

93 Avenida de Cervantes
Madrid

May 1st

Dear Janice,

I realise I am neither a woman of reason, nor ever likely to be a good Jewish housewife. I've been seeking the wrong advice entirely. From now on I'm going to be only what I am, and make the most of what I am. That is the way women succeed, not by trying to run a marriage as though it were a service industry, only to be offered early retirement because the job can be done more satisfactorily by some blonde *ingenue.* (She *is* blonde, by the way. Tom went spying for me. Good legs too – the bitch.)

So, how do I make the most of what I am? I believe I may have found the answer. I need a role model. I'm going to be like Jane Fonda. She was in Madrid this week, and I met her at a reception. Now, there's a woman who would know how to deal with Piers. She'd despatch tweetie-pie in ten seconds flat, and there wouldn't even be a spot of blood, just a puff of dust. How Piers might enjoy those muscled arms I'm not entirely sure: he says the woman looks like a cross between a Barbie Doll and

Arnold Schwarzenegger. The point is, though, Jane is older than I am, a hell of a lot older. Yet one glance at her and you realise age has nothing to do with it. Self-confidence is what does it, plus terrific radiant health. Jane positively bursts with it; it's a lethal weapon; that body is like a conquering army. And so shall mine be.

It isn't too bad as it is: I've just been having another look. I've got long legs, big breasts, and my hair looks good on the pillow (or so men tell me).

But then I take another look, and I say to myself 'No, Jane Fonda, you wouldn't approve, would you?' There's the hint of flab round the middle (fund-raising lunches), thighs that wobble a tiny bit (lack of employment); and those pectoral muscles, they could do with tightening up. You see, it's not properly in tune, my body; like a well-designed car in need of a service. I could do better. I need to remember that at thirty-six it's downhill all the way from now onwards unless I do something about it *now*.

Thank you, Jane. You shall be my mentor, my avatar – a good word, avatar, isn't it? The dictionary says, 'Descent of deity to earth in incarnate form.' Well, I shall emulate my deity until my own 'incarnate form' becomes very carnate indeed, an object of amazed and unswerving admiration. Piers Conway, you won't want to give your bit of stuff another glance once I've finished. The mature female form will triumph. I shall be the Flo-Jo of the diplomatic track.

All this may sound ridiculous to you as you slice prosciutto in your deli. But it's all very well, my Botticelli Venus; your body will always be petite and lovely. The

Creator did a mean job on you; he went to town on me. I could be all sacks and blue veins before I'm forty. Now is the moment to act.

I am going shopping.

Later.

Mixed success.

The Jane Fonda philosophy doesn't seem to have caught on in Madrid: I couldn't find her book anywhere, in any language. Nor could I find Rosemary Conley's *Hip and Thigh Diet* – though God knows some of the hips and thighs in the Gran Via could do with it. The British Council library would certainly have a copy, but I baulked at sidling up to tweetie-pie with an, 'Excuse me, I'm your lover's wife; I wonder if I might borrow Rosemary Conley's slimming book, you skinny little tart.'

The English bookshop did have something called *The Health and Beauty Workbook* by a certain Joy Slivovits (which I always thought was the name of a plum-brandy you buy in Yugoslavia: furthermore, to judge from her photograph she seemed a joyless and unbeautiful lady in rather poor health). However it was Hobson's Choice, so I purchased Ms Joyless Plum-brandy's workbook and have now flipped through it. There's a chapter entitled 'Body Mass', which seems a crude way of describing my luscious curves. 'Tasty Toxins' is the first sub-head: all the delicious things I absolutely mustn't eat and drink. I pursued this one carefully just in case there was something delicious I could slip to tweetie-pie to give her permanent diarrhoea. There wasn't. Then follows a section called 'Fats'. This is what it says: 'Fat deposits on the hips and thighs in women can lead to the traditional pear-shaped figure.' Well, mine isn't traditionally pear-shaped at all. It's traditionally rounded and voluptuous. Perhaps Ms Plum-brandy will make it even more so.

Then it's on to 'Stretching Exercises', with accompanying illustrations apparently smuggled out of an Iraqi torture-chamber. The text is more gentle. 'Go as far as you can into a squat without raising your heels.' That's easy enough, I do it every morning in the loo. After that it's 'Relaxation techniques'. This is a really weird one: 'Tighten every muscle in your face as if you are trying to touch your nose with your face.' I'd always imagined my nose *was* part of my face. Well, now I know. It goes on: 'Now stretch your face open and stick your tongue out as far as it will go. Relax.' Relax! How could I possibly relax with my face stretched enough to split and my tongue thrust out like a lollipop? Another one to skip.

The next section is headed 'Scoring'. Well! 'If less than once a month', she explains, 'then score a "No". "Yes" should mean at least once a week.' My answer has to be 'Normally "Yes", but at present definitely "No".' Ah – I see; over the page 'scoring' refers to a 'Thyroid metabolism questionnaire' – 'Are you constipated?' is the first question.

Janice, I don't think I can go on with this.

But just a minute; here's a section on 'Toning Exercises'. I like the idea of being 'toned'. Here's what Ms Plum-brandy advises: 'Walking briskly is a wonderful toning exercise. Other acceptable methods are – jogging, swimming, skipping, dancing, active sports, and the use of indoor machines.'

Do you think a vibrator counts as an indoor machine?

I have a feeling Lady Joyless might not consider the 'tone' of this letter quite appropriate. But she has given me a few ideas. I intend to jog along the Gran Via and on to the Retiro Gardens (the magnolias are in flower – white porcelain cups; I long to fill them with wine). I shall acquire an indoor exercise bike. And I shall seek out a local health club. I'm not sure about Ms Plum-brandy, but Jane Fonda is going to be proud of me.

It's May. Only seventy-two days to go. And a new page on the sun-tan calendar. This month the girl is more like me than tweetie-pie, I like to think; at least she's more like the woman I *shall* be when I'm 'toned' and exercised and in amazing health. My God, if I end up with tits like that they'll be queuing up, and Piers may just find he's at the very end of the queue. Serve him bloody well right.

I've decided to go and spend a night or two with the wondrous Estelle. I could do with a dose of that sharp Gallic mind, and the comfort of all Extremadura spreading around me. I'll ring her – at the right time of day.

My mean tricks on Piers fell flat. The pornography and paedophilia books got translated by that Spanish cretin into 'philosophy' and 'photography'. Piers mentioned it casually in passing. I said, 'How strange.' And the sculpture ended up as a wall of a multi-storey car park. Serves me right for playing childish games.

Two more fund-raising lunches this week. Money trickles in to support the conquistadors. Esteban is doing his best to become one.

As for you, I laughed aloud at your deli experiences.

Thank you for keeping me in touch with the lighter side of life. Your cable was a welcome surprise too. I'm glad something other than indigestion may emerge from my efforts at *haute cuisine.* You may have the Prawnography book idea with my love and blessing. I'm sure your artistic gifts will make the most of 'prawn cocktails' and the like. Who is going to write it? You're certainly not going to ask me. In any case I shall be far too busy transforming myself into May's calendar girl on whom the sun never sets and to whom every man rises.

Janice, this has to be the worst time in my life. I'm sometimes amazed I can fight and laugh. But what else can I do? – except write to you in friendship, knowing you are on my side.

With so much love,

Ruth.

1 River Mews

May 5th

Dearest Ruth,

Do be sure not to emulate Jane Fonda too closely: she's said to have had a rib surgically removed to narrow her waist. In your case that would be taking bimbo-bashing too far. You have a staggering figure as it is – Tom never stops talking about it, the rat. Do you remember that competition we had at school when we were about thirteen? Some ghastly girl challenged the class and we all had to submit to tape-measures. I was still flat as a board except for two acorns and got the booby prize, so to speak. You won amid envious gasps.

Now, glowing health – that's quite another matter. I would have thought jogging along the Gran Via might result in nothing healthier than lead-poisoning or the casualty ward. As for health clubs, the only time I went to one I thought I'd called in at the local *abattoir* by mistake: imagine an E.C. butter-mountain and you have it. Personally I'd stick to swimming and exercises. Have you noticed, by the way, how exercises described in health books can invariably be read as instructions for the 'thirty-nine positions'? I owe this piece of information to Kevin, who's something of an expert in these matters. I was foolish enough to let this slip in front of Tom, who nearly blew a gasket. 'You mean that appalling man's been your lover?' he burbled. 'Only once or twice,' I replied. He was almost apoplectic. 'Kevin!' he spluttered. 'The porno-king! You said "Yes" to him and "No" to me – a respectable and terribly famous Fleet Street hack. Who else?' I laughed. 'A few,' I said. 'How many?' he insisted, glaring at me, 'apart from your ex-husband.' 'Eight,' I answered precisely. 'You mean you *counted*?' I nodded sweetly. 'I had to,' I said.

I didn't say any more, and neither did Tom: he was too gobsmacked. Ruth, I really have become an appalling prick-teaser. But I'm scared of getting entangled with a man who's had five wives plus just about every woman I know. They're forever telling me, the swines. He doesn't; and when pressed puts on his helpless look and says, 'Well, you know how it is sometimes.' 'Yes, I *do* know,' I retort; 'you're a famous fucker.' 'And you, of course, are

Miss Virtue,' he replies, to which I say, 'No, but I'm scarcely in double figures; you're probably in treble.' The bastard has the nerve not even to deny it.

I bleed for you about the cooking disasters. The trouble is, you made it all sound so hilarious it was hard to grasp how agonising the evening must have been. Tom told me about it ever so discreetly, but when I showed him your letter (you don't mind, do you?) he said, 'Yes, I'm afraid it was a bit like that.' Then he added that you were looking stunning and Piers behaved like an absolute prat. Tom also said you were quite magnificent at the Queen's Birthday bunfight, and that the reports in the papers did you no justice at all. 'She's an empress, that woman,' he added dreamily.

Jesus, why should I be contemplating going to bed with a man who thinks you're an empress?

He then said wryly that Harry was getting into hot water with a senator's wife in Washington. 'What's new?' I asked. And he laughed. 'Hot water literally,' he explained. The lady apparently has a double bath (as distinct from a bubble bath). Well, at least it's a change from the water-bed he used to share with Ah-man-dah.

I sent you that cable about Prawnography because I was flabbergasted and couldn't get you on the phone. Let me tell you what happened. It began with Tom cooking me his long-promised Moroccan *tajine.* The flat was filled with the smell of saffron and coriander, and he produced a wonderful earthenware dish with a conical lid like a Chinese coolie hat which he'd bought at the souk in Marrakesh, he explained. Tom, I have to say, is a seriously great cook. As sweetmeat after sweetmeat appeared I began to daydream about myself as a *poule de luxe* reclining naked on extravagant cushions like one of Ingres's odalisques. Tom, it seemed, had much the same idea: this became obvious the moment he produced a lamb dish whose name he proudly translated for me from the Arabic as 'Virgins' Thighs'. At least he had the good grace to laugh. 'I appreciate you may not be one,' he said, 'but please allow me my fantasies.' 'Would you really prefer me to be a virgin?' I asked. 'Jesus, No,' he replied; 'I'd be terrified.'

We both laughed. I like him.

I liked him too when I asked if he always thought of his cooking as an aphrodisiac, and he answered with an absurdly straight face, 'I prefer to think it's my mind.'

It was at that point when I told him about your Prawnography idea. Tom lit up. Waved his arms in the air. 'Marvellous. A bedside cook-book on shell-fish. It's a winner. Please may I write it if you do the illustrations? I know exactly the man to publish it. I'll ring him tomorrow. We'll make a fortune – and have a great deal of fun.' And he leapt to his feet to open another bottle of wine. 'Think what one could do with cockles!' he went on. 'Or undressed prawns! There must be dozens of things you can do with prawns.' 'Dozens at least,' I said. 'What about Prawns *Soixante-Neuf*?' Tom looked at me amazed. I believe I actually shocked him for a moment. But he's an old hand, and recovered quickly. 'I think that might need researching.' 'Maybe,' I said cautiously. 'But with shell-fish doesn't there have to be an "r" in the month? And this is May.' He gave a belly-laugh. '*Touché*!'

The games we play, Ruth. Games that lead us round

and round what we're not sure if we want or not. They're a sort of testing-ground. Will I, won't I, will I, won't I, will I join the dance?

Not that evening I didn't. The phone went. It was obviously a girlfriend. Tom clearly wanted to murder her and be polite at the same time. I had half a mind to unzip his flies while he was talking. But then he answered 'Yes' just a few too many times, and by the time he rang off I was feeling distinctly cool. 'I suppose you're going to tell me that was your recently-divorced wife?' I remarked. 'No,' he said a little wearily, 'it was the wife before that.' *Touché*!

The next day Tom phoned me at the deli to say he'd spoken to his publisher friend, who badly wanted to meet me. He loved the idea, Tom assured me; could certainly sell it in the States provided it included freshwater clams. Germany too. Possibly France. Scandinavia without a doubt. A mayonnaise firm might even sponsor it if I could find a suitable use for salad cream. It would all depend on my illustrations. 'I told him you were brilliant,' Tom said. 'I'm sure you are, even though I've never seen a thing you've done. He's going to ring you at home. Try and have something to show him. He's very, very married, by the way, or I'd never have risked introducing you to him – for my sake, not yours.'

Then Tom added – 'His name is Samuel Johnson, and that's *not* a joke.'

The man did ring, yesterday evening, and his name *is* Samuel Johnson. He's coming round in a couple of weeks when I'll have something ready for him. So this weekend Janice Blakemore is going to coax her imagination into the realms of soft Prawnography. It'll certainly make a change from painting Shakespeare Country for American oil-tycoons, or weighing out half a pound of Continental Roast. Let's hope the Creepy Crawleys don't decide to forgive me my sins with a social call just as I'm undressing a prawn.

The only other news concerns Clive. What am I supposed to make of my prodigy of a twelve-year-old? For the Wigmore Hall he's chosen to play Bartok's solo violin sonata. 'Yehudi Menuhin originally commissioned it,' he explained nonchalantly; 'but I believe I can play it better.' The little monster then cut a rehearsal to go off to a cricket match at the Oval to watch Attila the Gun. He came back in mid-afternoon saying the match was over. I don't understand a thing about cricket, but Clive showed me what he called a 'score-card', and it did suggest the opposition hadn't done all that well. 'What's "rtd ht" mean?' I asked. He nodded. 'Attila's a very dangerous bowler. Middlesex only made thirty-one runs. Now they're mostly in hospital.' And he grinned.

Why did I think cricket was a sport for gentlemen?

Shall I send you health food parcels from Ching's deli? We do a nice line in *foie gras aux truffes.* And clotted cream would go down a treat with your Scandakrisp wafers.

Good luck.

And huge love,

Janice (By Appointment, Limner to the catering trade).

Palacio Pizarro
Trujillo

May 10th

Dear Janice,

Things achieved:

– I've jogged through the Madrid rush-hour in the spring rain.

– I've gorged myself sick on crispbreads that taste like old matchboxes.

– I've replaced alcohol with burpy mineral-water, nicotine with chewing-gum, sugar with Sweetex.

– I've joined a health club whose members resemble Marlene Dietrich in decline.

– I've acquired a refined instrument of torture called a Nautilus exercise machine.

– I've lost precisely *two* pounds – Oh God! But each morning I look at my sun-tan calendar and say, 'I'll get there, I'll get there.'

– I ache, am bruised, am hungry, am filthy-tempered, am not at all sure Piers is worth all this sweat.

– I've discovered the little tart's name is Angelica. It would be, wouldn't it? Angelica. The little angel. Flutter, flutter. Piers, fly me. Yuk!

– I've rebelled. Escaped. I have a hangover *chez* the wise and wicked Estelle. And all of a sudden life feels one hell of a lot better. Just for this weekend Ms Joyless Plum-brandy can cry into her muesli. I'm having fun.

Beyond my key-hole window spreads Extremadura, green turning gold already, outcrops of granite protruding like old knuckles. The storks are familiar friends, clack-clacketting their bills around the rooftops of the town square. A café-owner recognised me. So did a three-legged dog: it was a rear-leg missing. I became intrigued to know how it would either cock a leg that wasn't there, or fall over. So I followed it, but it didn't oblige. The café-owner followed *me*: he looked more interested in cocking a leg than the dog.

I love it here. It's not my world, but it's one I can slide into very easily. Even as I write, some *chico* is probably wax-polishing the white Mercedes. Xavier heard I was coming, and provided. I'd earned it, he said: the conquistador collection is growing apace. We are promised the head of Montezuma; I assume a hoax, or else some confusion with John the Baptist (the Spaniards will believe anything miraculous). In any case, all last week I clobbered my withdrawal symptoms with various kinds of fund-raising razzamatazz. I oozed happiness, charm and persuasiveness. 'Your Excellency is a wonderful woman,' I was told. 'Señor Conway is a lucky man' (too right he is: he's got a young mistress). Esteban shadowed me silently, and one evening took me out to dinner and again informed me how beautiful his hacienda was at this time of the year. I was praying he wasn't going to say 'almost as beautiful as you', but I'm afraid he did. The man is a gorgeous cliché – gorgeous none the less. He is one of those men who should never be allowed to open his mouth, only look darkly and thereby appear irresistibly interesting, mainly in bed. Silence can be a potent aphrodisiac, though not one I've ever managed to master.

Now – Estelle.

I was summoned for lunch. Conscious of her Duchess of Windsor mood of the mornings I dressed smartly. She was by the pool, naked as usual, and reading. She didn't raise her head, and began to talk as though I'd been with her since my last visit nearly two months ago. Perhaps she believed I had.

'I've made a discovery, my dear,' she announced, still not taking her eyes off her book. 'Your predicament has set me thinking about the English, and why we French find it so hard to understand you, and you us.' For the first time she looked up at me. 'Good God, you're dressed for a garden party. Why don't you remove those things and take a dip while I talk. Miguel will bring some wine in a minute, unless you prefer something disgusting like *sangria*.'

It sounded like an order, so I cautiously undressed. I could see no sign of Miguel, whoever he might be: last time it had been Luis. I decided to dive into the pool quickly, realising only just in time that it was the shallow end, then walked as nonchalantly as I could to the far end. It seemed to take an awfully long time.

'Magnificent body you have, my dear,' Estelle called out. 'My first husband adored breasts like yours. I'm afraid I disappointed him. But then he disappointed me in every other respect. Now, about my discovery.'

The water came as a cool shock, and when I surfaced Estelle was seating herself by the edge of the pool, legs dangling in the water, a book in either hand. Her body was as brown as a walnut. I swam gently up and down while she talked.

'Yes, the difference between the English and the

French. Simple: it's here in these two books.' And she held them both up in front of her. I couldn't read the titles. 'It's a question of upbringing, my dear,' she went on. 'Your children are brought up on A.A. Milne – *Winnie the Pooh* and such. Ours are brought up on the *Fables* of La Fontaine.'

Estelle paused to contemplate a fly which had settled on her left breast, before flicking it away like a waiter brushing a crumb from the table. I swam another length waiting for her to continue her dissertation.

'La Fontaine is admirable, of course,' she went on. 'He delights the child, the student of poetry, and the scholar. He has depth of understanding and subtlety of thought. What we owe to him is immeasurable. He has made us what we are. As a result we French are witty, clever and sharp.' She paused to attack another fly, then put down La Fontaine and instead waved A.A. Milne in my direction. I stopped swimming and clung to the rail, waiting for her grand conclusion. I didn't think the Brits were going to come out of this particularly well. 'I ask you,' she said, 'how could any Frenchman possibly understand a nation brought up to emulate a teddy-bear called Pooh?' With that she began to recite. '"Lines written by a bear of very little brain." "On Monday when the sun is hot, I wonder to myself a lot: Now is it true, or is it not, that what is which, and which is what?"'

Estelle snapped the book closed, and laughed. 'Don't you see, my dear; your bear of very little brain has managed to express perfectly in four lines what the philosopher Spinoza failed to articulate in a dozen or more volumes – namely, the nature of oneness and human individuality?'

I started to say something perplexed, but Estelle hadn't finished. She stood up and stretched her naked form to the sun. 'What I mean,' she went on, declaiming to all Extremadura spread below us, 'we French are simple people taught to be clever, while you English are clever, taught to be simple.' She lowered her book. 'Ah, here's Miguel with the wine.'

I rippled the pool urgently to disguise my nakedness from the young man who was approaching with a silver tray in his hand and a napkin over one arm. Estelle thanked him in Spanish and took the tray from him. He seemed to find nothing odd about serving wine to two naked females, but I went on rippling the pool until he'd gone. Then I got out and began to dry myself on Estelle's towel.

So why, I asked her, had my 'predicament' – as she put it – made her think about *Winnie the Pooh* and La Fontaine? What had her 'discovery' revealed to her about myself?

She looked at me sharply. 'Goals,' she said. 'What people aim for. Because you're taught to be simple, you value simple feelings – sentiments. We French are taught to be clever, and sentiment is *not* clever, so we don't value it: only the deeper feelings – passion, hatred, lust. Your attachment to your tiresome husband is all sentiment, which is why I have such a struggle to understand it. The clever thing to do, of course, would be to make him even more jealous than you are.' She clicked her fingers in the direction of the terrace. 'Miguel,' she called out. 'My clothes, if you please.' She turned back to me. 'The sun is too hot for my old skin. My breasts wrinkle like figs. How lucky you are to be still ripe, my dear.'

'And who is Miguel?' I asked. 'It used to be Luis.' Estelle poured out two glasses of white wine. 'Luis is on leave of absence for a while. He got married,' she explained. 'Miguel is his brother. I like to keep it in the family – I think one always should with servants.' She sipped her wine and looked reflective. 'Poor Luis, he'll be having a miserable time. The girl's a virgin, of course. Terribly clumsy, I'm sure. However, soon she'll be pregnant and then he won't have to bother her for a long while. I do miss him. Miguel is, as they say, only a "stand-in", and he has much to learn. Do refresh your glass. It's a wine the King particularly likes, but I'm refusing to sell him the vineyard. It must be the only time I've ever said "No" to a king.'

Miguel re-appeared bearing a small pile of clothes, neatly folded. Then he returned a few moments later with a tray of cold lunch. Estelle gave him a dismissive nod of thanks.

'I'm beginning to tire of sex,' she announced as she passed me a plate of sea-food salad. (People do choose their moments.) 'I wish there were something more suitable to old age that wasn't bridge or drink,' she went on. Then she laughed. 'I could be like you English, of course, and become ridiculous about dogs, but even bad sex might be more interesting than that. You see' – and she gazed wistfully down at her naked body – 'the Lord gave us such limited resources; just in and out, in and out all the time. But then since God restricted himself to creating only one pair of prototypes he would naturally have been more anxious about procreation than pleasure, wouldn't he? It seems to have worked too, judging by the traffic-jams in Madrid. All the same, supposing Adam had been homosexual: have you ever considered that? We wouldn't be here, my dear. We have to be very thankful to the serpent.'

There was a pause while Estelle took in these thoughts. She reached for an apricot, but decided against it in favour of a cigarette and another glass of wine. Then she pulled on a T-shirt and a minute pair of pants. The T-shirt had a garish bullfighting scene on the front, and '*Olé*' splashed beneath it. Estelle saw my look of surprise. 'Luis bought it for me on his honeymoon. I like it: it's vulgar, and so am I. All aristocrats are. Refinement is for the bourgeoisie. Now,' and she gave me another of her sharp looks, 'before I take my siesta I want to know whether you've slept with my nephew Esteban yet.' I said I hadn't. 'A pity,' she said. 'I was hoping you'd tell me all about it this evening at dinner. I may be tired of sex, but I'm not tired of hearing about it. Besides, it interests me to know what he's like. And as a woman of sentiment you'd have told it well. Esteban is beautiful, isn't he? But beautiful men are often so bad at it, I find. Cary Grant was like that.'

Estelle is good at exit lines.

I knew the siesta would stretch into the evening, so as the day began to cool I took the car out for an hour. The roof was down, and the air full of bees and bird-song. I came across a stream that clattered among rocks between pools where frogs plopped from the reed-beds. Horses were standing in the water, swishing their tails and gazing at me with sad eyes. Mottled hills rose all about me, and an eagle was soaring. It was intensely beautiful and lonely. I suddenly wished Piers could have been there with me. These were the kinds of moment that cemented our marriage, moments when nothing needed saying. I felt angry. 'What a fool,' I said out loud: 'he may miss this for ever.' And if this is sentiment, I thought, I value it above being clever.

But then I never quite believe Estelle. She's too warm not to love what she claims to despise. In her own way I think she envies what I feel for Piers, which is why she takes such extravagant pains not to understand. But what a woman! I re-enacted our naked lunch for you in order to give you a cameo of her. She has an inexhaustible capacity to entertain, merely by being what she is.

Over dinner I told her about my health and beauty regime, and of course she laughed. 'But you have both already, my dear. As for exercise, life is an exercise. What's the use of developing muscles fit for a weight-lifter when all you need is to be able to pick up a glass of wine?' And she refilled mine. There was no way I could explain, so I let her talk, which is what she really likes to do. She was in a contemplative mood. Did I think she had wasted her life? she asked me at one point. It was a rhetorical question. 'If so,' she went on, 'I've had enormous fun wasting it, and intend to continue doing so.' I reminded her of the millions she'd raised for charity, the *Légion d'Honneur*, etc. '*Honneur*,' she snorted. 'It was mostly *déshonneur*: I fucked heads of state. As for charity, most of that got wasted too. Charity is a kind of open drain. In the old days we built cathedrals; now we give to Oxfam. I know which I'd prefer. The epitaph on my tombstone shall read

"Estelle, Marquésa de Trujillo y Toledo, who wasted her life and loved it.'"

A minute later she fell asleep at the table. Miguel quietly carried her from the room. It was two o'clock in the morning.

Now the morning has almost gone. All is silence *chez Estelle.* Maybe at this very moment she is turning her attention to Eeyore and Tigger: what philosophical revelations will emerge today? Heaven help us when she moves on to Roald Dahl.

A stork has just flapped past my window bearing a squirming tit-bit of the kind Ms Joyless Plum-brandy would probably recommend for my health-lunch. Ah well! Tomorrow it's the Nautilus exercise machine with a vengeance.

Meanwhile, the best of luck with Tom and the prawns. Avoid crabs.

With much love,

Ruth.

93 Avenida de Cervantes
Madrid

May 10th

Dear Harry,

I regret you won't be part of the Presidential entourage when he meets E.C. leaders here next week, but naturally I understand your first duty is to comfort the senator's wife while foreign affairs commitments detain him in Europe. You have always been unusually kind-hearted in these matters.

Alas, I've never had the experience of a double bath, but I'm happy to take your word for it that the missionary position is not recommended.

Your gratuitous verses on the theme of lady librarians struck me as imaginative and in your customary poor taste. On a point of information, only French books have uncut pages: this is Spain. And as far as I'm aware, the author of *The Lays of Ancient Rome* never did write a sequel on Madrid, and if so it was certainly not published by Mills and Boon. Angelica's reading is actually rather scholarly. She has every intention of applying for Maidstone Polytechnic to study art history and comparative religions.

No, my sense of humour does *not* desert me every time I mention her. Perhaps I had better not do so in future since your own dives for the gutter whenever I do. And I wish you would stop referring to her as my 'child mistress'. Angelica is a mature and responsible woman, and definitely not my mistress, as you well know.

Ruth has disappeared for the weekend with a dypsomaniac *marquésa,* leaving behind an extraordinary wrapped object described on the label as Nautilus. Isn't that some kind of deep-sea creature with a shell, and what might she possibly want with such a thing? I dread its unveiling. Or perhaps in a fit of enthusiasm she's acquired one of the pieces of contemporary British sculpture I was compelled to enthuse about publicly a short while ago. I suppose Ruth may have thought I meant it. If so our next dinner-party should be livelier than the last.

I shall have to greet the PM when he arrives for the E.C. conference. I trust the issue of Gibraltar won't arise, and that monkeys form no part of Ruth's welcoming conversation. In the company of politicians her imagination is easily roused, and less easily calmed.

Life is not easy on several fronts at present. I'm looking forward to introducing Angelica to the El Grecos in Toledo once this E.C. fandango is over. She has such a hunger for works of art. To me, she is one.

As a matter of interest, how *do* you do it in the bath?

All the best,

Piers.

Porthmeor Hotel
St Ives
Cornwall

May 17th

Dear Slimline,

I do not approve of health. I would never have reached the age of fifty-five had I kept a check on my diet, my weight, my blood-pressure, my alcohol intake; if I'd chewed multi-vitamins, jogged, done press-ups, had eight hours sleep a night, munched ginseng and organic vegetables, and greeted each dawn with Tai-Chi. So why should you, at the tender age of thirty-six, fall victim to soul-crushing regimes? And for no better cause than to win back the heart of a husband who's not remotely worthy of you? Why don't you just leave him to his foolish dream, enjoy a freedom which you've always insisted on anyway, and then lend him a Kleenex to dry his tears when the dream shatters?

I believe I met your friend Estelle once, I can't remember where. I have a feeling Biarritz was part of the scenario, but the circumstances elude me. Maybe it's as well. No point asking her: she was probably with some king or other, and wouldn't recall an uncouth newshound sniffing around her skirts.

An absurd story brings me here to this outpost of the known world. An art faker. Oh God, who cares? As far as I can see they're all art fakers down here: colonies of them in French designer denims and open sandals, bitching each other up like crazy and reversing the charges to their London dealers. Even their pictures all look the same, as if they started out quite nice and then the tide came in. But, as you know, I'm an ignoramus in these matters. People like me said the same about Gauguin. I probably still would.

Janice has doubtless told you I found her a publisher for your Prawnography idea – a certain Samuel Johnson (haven't I heard that name somewhere before?). We collaborate well, Janice and I. As master-chef I cook her seductive delicacies, which don't have the desired effect but do feed her imagination quite amazingly. She refuses to show me her illustration for Fresh-water Clams in Extra Virgin Olive Oil until it's finished. That woman is seriously dangerous. And if Dr Johnson is as good as his word she'll also be seriously rich. And if she is, so shall I. Perhaps we shall both end up down here in farthest Cornwall enjoying the pseuds' life; even opening a sea-food restaurant of marvellous pretentiousness, draped with fishing-nets and lobster pots, and serving prawnographic food on neolithic plates of the Bernard Leach school.

Seriously, shall I ask her to marry me?

Does she say terrible things about me? She certainly says terrible things *to* me. I think I could love her, but I'm not sure she knows what the word means.

No librarian's assistant called Angelica is to be taken seriously. I've had much experience of angels, and they have no substance – unlike you, dear Ruthless.

To whom, much love,

Tom.

Hospital de la Misericordia
Madrid

May 19th

Dear Janice,

Fifty-five days remaining.

Marital Repairs Service Report No 3

It's not easy writing this lying flat and propelling my biro upwards: the ink won't be dissuaded from obeying the law of gravity, and neither will the blood in my arms. So I shall attempt this letter in short bursts.

The nurses are confident I should be able to go home tomorrow provided they can get me vertical.

Right now I can't even reach the telephone, and the only view from where I lie is of a spider who traverses the ceiling rather as I traversed the floor when Piers brought me here.

The quality of life improved once Estelle delivered superlative wine of the kind she normally sends only to the King. I'm not sure I should be drinking it through one of those wiggly plastic straws that look like a transparent French horn, but it was the only kind my resourceful husband could locate – in a children's joke-shop. My first attempt to embibe had been from a leather calabash-thing – you know, the sort Spanish shepherds carry round their necks on the sierras, and English tourists bring back in plane-loads from the Costa del Sol with semi-naked gypsies painted on them. The trouble is, you need to be able to aim. I can't. The wall of my hospital room looked as if someone's brains had been blown out. The straw is a distinct improvement, though having the wine go round and round the plastic tubing before it reaches my lips probably does terrible things to the *bouquet*; and I'm not sure Piers thinks it's quite commensurate with the dignity of a Chargé d'Affaires' wife.

Do I make it sound as though the bastard's returned penitent and loving to my side? Not on your bloody life he has. True, he visits me with guilty flowers and embarrassed condolences; then he goes off free as air to spend romantic nights with tweetie-pie, who may indeed be pinned on her back rather like me though with something more stimulating than Estelle's wine to keep her warm, the bitch.

So, you'd like to know how I did it. Well, it was that fucking Nautilus exercise machine. Returning from Estelle's I got down to it in earnest. I rode the thing. I pedalled. I strained. It teased out every muscle and spun it taut as a coiled spring. The bathroom resounded to my grunts and urgings: no room for Piers to stand on his head any more, thank heaven. I could feel my thighs becoming lissom, my stomach as smooth as a drum, my breasts upright and proud as a brace of guardsmen. Oh Jane Fonda, you should have seen me. I glanced contemptuously at my sun-tan calendar and said 'you flabby weed'. And I thought: 'Piers Conway, after your skinny little tart this body is going to drive you wild.' I could hear him gasping in amazement and joy: 'Don't stop, don't stop: devour me.' And just when he thought he couldn't do it any more, I'd flex my pectorals and rotate my hips, and he'd be raised in helpless lust until I finally released him from his agony as a limp and sated rag-doll, fighting for breath and swamped in tears of gratitude.

Do I make any of this sound plausible? Again, I'm afraid I mock where I should weep.

It was the morning the Prime Minister was due to arrive. Piers was selecting the sort of clothes a PM might expect to be met in. I was enjoying my morning work-out with Nautilus and between grunts making helpful suggestions like – 'How about your white topee, dear? And that grass skirt you were presented with in Tonga – it would look good with your M.C.C. tie. You could take Angelica along with an ivory hoop through her nose and introduce her as your native bride.'

None of this went down frightfully well, I have to say: Piers was in a mood for fussing about collar-studs. I said I'd seen the fucking things here in the bathroom – 'Over there!' And as I pointed 'over there' a terrible crunch savaged my back. It was too painful even to cry out. My mouth fell open. I froze. Nautilus held me up.

Have you ever seen those figures in Pompeii, petrified in mid-action as the volcanic ash buried them? Well, that was me. I was motionless, speechless, trapped on Nautilus. I gurgled: it was all I could do. Piers found his collar-studs and gazed at me, puzzled. 'You're very silent all of a sudden,' he said rather crossly. 'Anything the matter?' I found one part of me that worked – my neck. I nodded, and gurgled again. I went on nodding. Then I found a teeny bit of my voice. 'My back,' I whispered. 'It's gone. I'm paralysed – for life.'

Even then I found the imagination to exaggerate.

I shall now describe to you the rest of the nightmare. Somehow, inch by inch, I released myself from the clutches of Nautilus. I was on the floor, sort of sideways in a lump. Piers decided gentle massage was the answer. It was the wrong answer. I yelled. At that moment Teresa our maid arrived, white as a sheet. She obviously imagined she'd walked in on an attempted murder. But to her eternal credit Teresa has grown accustomed to our oddities, and didn't throw a wobbly or rush screaming into the street calling on Holy Mary Mother of Jesus. She grasped the situation and immediately knew what to do. She gradually eased me into lying flat on my back, placed books under my feet to raise them and flatten the arch of my back, then slipped a pillow under my head. Most important of all, she shoo'd Piers out of the bathroom like a hen that had strayed in from the farmyard. 'Woman's work,' she announced. That gave me my first moment of pleasure. I found voice enough to add my own tuppence-worth: 'Do something useful, Piers; stand on your head, or something,' I murmured. He departed fiddling with his collar-studs and mumbling about the Prime Minister.

Of course I should have left him to it. He didn't need me to accompany him – least of all as a paralytic. But you know how it is when you realise you're not really about to die: you decide nothing is wrong at all – it's perfectly all right, don't make such a fuss, stop treating me like an invalid and bloody well SHUT UP. Piers should have *shut* me up. He didn't. He stood around looking miserable and glancing at his watch while the maid – patiently and tenderly – got me dressed. I was determined to be on that tarmac with Piers when the PM descended: he was my husband, the Chargé d'Affaires, and I was going to be seen to be his wife; and if Spanish television recorded the event I hoped the British Council library had a TV set and that tweetie-pie would be loyally watching it.

I managed the stairs down from the flat. I managed the car, both in and out. I managed the walk from the VIP lounge towards the plane, slowly but steadily. Ramrod upright I was. The plane taxied to a halt. Dignitaries and their wives gathered: medals, gloves, hats, handbags just like our dear Queen, polite coughing, smoothing of hair in the wind, hands clasped behind backs, press photographers hovering. Piers was right there at the front, by protocol the first to welcome the visitor; and me by his side. I've not often felt proud in the diplomatic circus-ring, but I did then. I felt proud of Piers, and proud *for* him. I felt confident that from now onwards everything was going to be all right. A little librarian's assistant suddenly seemed very small fry indeed – something to be brushed aside by the great sweep of history.

And there at the door of the aircraft was the man

himself, looking disconcertingly like his cartoons, but the Prime Minister none the less. He waved. He descended the steps. Piers took a pace forwards and shook the PM's hand. I felt a knighthood coming on. Then it was my turn. I took my own step forward – and crunch! I was down. I don't remember those moments too clearly. What I do know is that the Prime Minister of all England, Wales, Scotland and Northern Ireland (not to mention Gibraltar) was introduced to the wife of Her Britannic Majesty's Head of Mission on all fours.

As he tried to raise me to my feet I swear he murmured 'Dear Mrs Conway, this really isn't necessary.' He *is* very inexperienced, remember. But whatever may have been going through his head was certainly not going through mine. My only thought – and I despised myself even as I thought it – was that tweetie-pie would be watching this performance on television, confirmed in her view that her lover was married to a werewolf who should certainly be put down.

And now here I am. I have made the front pages of the national press for the second time in Piers' brief tenure of office. At the Hospital de la Misericordia the nurses are kind, the food is excellent if you don't mind eating paella flat on your back, and I'm growing quite fond of the spider. But tomorrow it's goodbye to all this, and goodbye to Jane Fonda, to Nautilus, to Ms Joyless Plum-brandy, to jogging, to diets, to health foods, and to all unlovely and punitive ways of living. And the girl in the sun-tan calendar can go fuck herself. If my boobs droop, they droop. If my thighs wobble, they wobble. Who the hell cares? Piers doesn't give a sod anyway, so why should I?

Why should I care about men at all? I'd rather spend my time with Estelle, and writing to you – next time I hope from an upright position.

Piers' upright position can look after itself.

How's Tom's?

'Oh, self-traitor, I do bring the spider love, which transubstantiates all, and can convert Manna to gall.'

I bet you don't know where that quote comes from? I do, but have no idea what it's supposed to mean. It just sticks in my head. I've been saying it aloud to my friendly spider, and he hasn't dropped on my head since.

Do you think I'm losing my mind?

Even if you do, I send you my love. And if ever I needed gossip from River Mews, it is now.

Ruth.

1 River Mews

May 25th

Dearest Ruth,

I was going to launch into telling you about Attila the Gun, but I'd hate to put your back out again. So I'll begin more gently with Samuel Johnson.

Tom told me to expect someone who was reserved, scholarly, very English, very proper and very married. Then why on earth, I asked, should such a man be interested in publishing *Prawnography*, and what's more be prepared to offer me a fat advance to do the illustrations? Tom laughed. 'You need to understand about Sam,' he said, and proceeded to tell me this story.

Samuel Johnson started a small publishing business seven or eight years ago, specialising in quaint little books on country folklore and local customs – the sort of thing you pick up in National Trust gift-shops along with the tea-towel and the bees-wax candles. One day a literary agent of blessed memory offered him a manuscript from the estate of an ancient and long-forgotten lady author: Sam was the last chance before the manuscript was to be returned to the grieving family. The title was *William comes to town*, and it was the story of a Victorian orphan who runs away to London where he's befriended/defrauded/exploited by a series of ladies in whose houses he seeks employment: 'A cross between Dickens and Dick Whittington,' as Tom put it.

Now, Sam's sales director is an old drinking companion of Tom's. Flogging books on country wines and Derbyshire well-dressing was beginning to drive him nuts, but with half the publishing trade joining the dole queue there was nowhere else to go. He had to make the best of it, even when it came to offering a professional opinion on *William comes to town*. The man groaned, downed a treble scotch, and read it in ten minutes. And in those ten minutes he had an idea. To post-Freudian ears the tearful and innocent story possessed undertones that were both humorous and extremely dubious – it was clearly a book about adolescent fantasy and sexual initiation. He recommended to Sam that it be given a snappier title – *Willy Nilly* – and be illustrated in a suitably post-Freudian manner. This was not quite how he put it to Sam; none the less an illustrator was found, the book in due course published under its new title, and within a matter of weeks the adventures of young Willy's willy became required cult reading. It remained on the bestseller list for three years, was translated into thirteen languages, and made a fortune for Sam and the estate of the lady-author.

'You see,' Tom explained, 'Sam is living proof of the axiom that publishers only ever get it right by accident.'

'But what about the illustrations?' I said. 'He must have understood those, surely. He can't be that innocent.'

Tom laughed again.

'There's one more thing I haven't told you about Sam,' he went on. 'He's as blind as a bat. Anything beyond three feet is a blur or a blob. He believes to this day that *Willy Nilly* made it as a literary masterpiece, an English classic. It's a bit like a manufacturer making a million out of children's party balloons without realising they're the best condoms on the market. That's how publishing works.'

The point of this tale, Tom assured me, is that the sales director has been looking for another jackpot ever since. And he believes *Prawnography* could be it – 'provided we can get it past Sam.'

'Precisely, Tom,' I said. 'So what about my illustrations? You've seen them. They're absolutely filthy.'

'That's OK,' said Tom. 'All you have to do is make sure he doesn't get within three feet of them.'

Well, I really didn't know what to do. The man was due to come round on Saturday evening after I got back from the deli. I'd been working all the previous weekend, every evening since then and half the night, producing stuff to show him on the assumption that he was the publisher's equivalent of Kevin the porno-movie king. Instead I was to be confronted with a half-blind innocent.

Tom merely wished me well and handed me the recipes to go with the water-colours I'd been making. 'Good luck,' he said.

Dear Ruth, please try to envisage the situation. What I'd been painting was 1) Prawns *Soixante-Neuf* 2) Fresh-water Clams in Extra Virgin Olive Oil, and 3) Mussel Tart with Basil. Without over-taxing your imagination it would be fair to say that the first is straight indecent, the second marginally less so, while the third depicts a certain Basil (who is not entirely unlike Harry) doing what comes naturally with a generously-endowed tart (who is not entirely unlike Ah-man-dah).

You see my predicament?

The doorbell rang. I quickly hid Prawns *Soixante-Neuf* in a drawer: not even a blind man could have mistaken what was going on there. A nervous, stooping figure entered, wearing a charcoal-grey suit within which he shrank. You could have mistaken him for a librarian's assistant (sorry!). His hair was thinning on top, but compensating generously on his hands. He was the sort of man who always cuts himself shaving: wisps of cotton-wool hung about his face. The smile was more a twitch than a smile. The handshake was bony and cool. It was hard to imagine him giving anyone an orgasm – not even himself. Perhaps he'd acquired his wife and children through myopia.

So this was Samuel Johnson, my samaritan.

I put him at his ease with a cup of tea: I could see

that the suggestion of anything stronger would have perturbed him.

'We are all of us most excited by your idea,' he began. I awarded him my Princess Di smile. 'In recent years we have enjoyed considerable success with illustrated books of a popular but serious nature,' he went on, holding his tea-cup before him like a priest bearing the host. 'My sales director assures me there is a distinct glamour in shell-fish. Your role, of course, will be to enhance that glamour.' He looked at me sharply, but remembering what Tom had told me about his eyesight I realised he probably could hardly see me at all. He put down his cup and leaned forwards confidentially. 'I understand from Mr Brand that you have done a great deal of work internationally in this sort of field.'

I blanched. What on earth had Tom told him? I thought of my major achievements as an artist. One mural for my son's bedroom. Another for my mother's loo. Another for a friendly neighbour down the road. A couple of freak commissions for American oil magnates. An even freakier one for Kevin. And one cancelled order from an Indian polo-rajah. And that was it. Did that add up to an international reputation? I needed a vodka and tonic, and poured myself one as discreetly as I could. I hoped Sam imagined it was Malvern water.

'Oh indeed,' I said; then, covering my tracks, 'of a varied kind. I generally work on a much larger scale, but I prefer not to specialise. One grows stale.'

Mr Johnson nodded. 'Quite so. Quite so. The imagination must be kept fresh. But perhaps you have something to show me. I should enjoy that. A new artist for us is always something of an adventure.'

I was shaking. Oh God, I thought, I hope Tom's right. Never closer than three feet, he warned me. I moved the easel out of the sunlight and smiled beatifically.

'A pleasure,' I said. 'Please do remain comfortably seated, Mr Johnson. I'll place them here: the colours will show up better against white, I think, and you'll get a sense of perspective. This is my first. The recipe is for Mussel Tart with Basil – a traditional Genoese dish, so Tom tells me. He's so very well-travelled. And of course he grows his own basil, as you know. The broad-leaved variety of course.'

Sam nodded again. I could see him screwing up his eyes. He appeared pleased. I felt confident enough to say something more.

'The idea, you see, is to animate the recipes with pictures that show people as if they might be anticipating the dish in question. Pictures of just food by itself do look awfully dead, wouldn't you agree? This one represents a couple – a married couple – expressing delight at what they're about to enjoy.' (Well, that was accurate anyway.)

'Very beautiful,' Sam said after a moment. And he tapped his fingers appreciatively. 'The pinks and reds will stand out well on the printed page.'

'That's very much what I hoped,' I added firmly.

Metaphorically I blew Tom a kiss. Then I replaced Basil and his tart with Fresh-water Clams in Extra Virgin Olive Oil. 'A New World recipe – from Baltimore,' I announced, by now quite myself. 'Fresh-water clams are famous there, as you know. Again, you see the human interest.'

Sam was beginning to look a very happy man. 'Quite lovely,' he was saying. 'The flesh tints. The curvilinear effect.'

And excitedly he rose, and began to cross the room.

'They deserve appreciating in detail,' he went on. 'I'm a little short-sighted, you know. And fresh-water clams are a particular favourite of mine, and of my dear wife.'

In a flash I was on guard. Never closer than three feet! I took a hasty step half in front of where the fresh-water clam was getting extremely fresh with the Extra Virgin, and hoped that Sam's sense of propriety would preserve a *cordon sanitaire* of at least two feet from me. I turned my breasts towards him as a further protective shield.

Sam stopped, screwed up his eyes and said again, 'Quite lovely. I hope you have more. I am enjoying this.'

'Well, do please be seated, Mr Johnson, and I'll pour you another cup of tea,' I said confidently. I daren't move away from the Extra Virgin until Sam was safely out of range.

A little reluctantly he sat down while I poured the tea. I was now in a dilemma. Dare I show him Prawns *Soixante-Neuf*? Oh, why not?, I thought. So I went over to the drawer and took out the water-colour I'd hidden there. Immediately Sam was on his feet again. Now I was caught: the easel was fully exposed across the room, and in my hand was a vivid demonstration of cunnilingus among the crustacea. Sam stood between me and the easel. Trusting to his blindness I kicked over a standard-lamp. Thank God the bulb broke. We were now in mercifully deep shadow.

'Never mind', I said. 'Let me show you as best I can.' And I placed Prawns *Soixante-Neuf* over the other two on the easel.

'This is a more complex design,' I explained. 'The idea is to suggest – symbolically you might say – what a great many ways there are of preparing prawns. Tom estimates there are no fewer than sixty-nine: would you believe it?' I paused for a couple of seconds to suggest profundity. 'So this is an illustration of an allegorical nature: the figures are so to speak floating: dreaming together, you could say. Sharing the delight of all those many methods.'

The pleasure on Sam's face was more radiant than ever.

'Indeed I do see. Very clever. And most tasteful, I may say: the figures reclining. We produced a handsome book recently on Titian's reclining figures. I'm reminded of it – without wishing to flatter you.'

'And that, I'm afraid, is all I've done so far,' I said regretfully. 'Though of course if you were interested . . .'

Sam interrupted my pause with a wave of the hand.

'I look forward to our collaboration,' he said. And he rose to his feet. 'Meanwhile I hope you'll accept this in advance of contract.'

And he produced from his jacket pocket a cheque which he handed to me. I looked at it. The Nat West cheque had a wren on it, and over the wren was written 'Pay Janice Blakemore or order the sum of five thousand pounds.' It was signed in neat handwriting, 'Samuel P. Johnson'.

'An honorarium,' he said. 'A gesture of my good faith.'

As he made his way to the door I just managed to remove the three water-colours from the easel before he squeezed past it. He stood awkwardly by the front door for a moment or two, thanking me several times and promising a confirming letter within days. And he would be doing the same with Mr Brand, for whom he had the deepest respect. Then he bid me goodbye with a little gesture of the hand as if he'd forgotten he was wearing no hat. I wished the Creepy Crawleys could have passed by in order to witness what respectable company I kept.

I poured myself another stiff vodka and tonic and gazed at the cheque until it began to blur. Then I phoned Tom to invite him to dinner at the Gavroche. The bastard was out. I left a tantalising message on his answering machine, and got drunk on scrambled eggs.

And that is the story so far of the Titian of River Mews. Ruth, I don't know much about publishing, but I know the publishers I like – the blind ones with cheque-books.

This means that I could now afford to give up Ching's Deli. Curiously I don't actually want to just yet. Being Titian is a lonely business, and the deli is becoming my social *salon.* It's surprising what confidences can be exchanged for a pound of coffee. I stand behind my shop counter like a *padre* hearing confession. Last year, when I was racing off the street, it was the husbands who confided in me about their wives. Now it's the wives – often the same wives – who confide in me about their husbands. And of course I already know, and they don't know it was me. Kindly picture the scene. 'That'll be £1.88p. It's 12p change, and thank you Louisa. I'm sure it'll work out all right. Ambrose always struck me as a kind and loving man. We all go through these little ups and downs, don't we?' Ambrose's ups and downs *were* rather little, as I recall. After Louisa left the deli yesterday I thought of another recipe for Tom: Winkles with Nuts – *in memoriam* Ambrose.

Events next-door have taken a surprising turn. I told you Kevin's wife had fled to the country, exhausted. Kevin's response has been to fall in love. 'No point waitin' around for you, Janice darlin',' he announced last week. The new girl's Vietnamese. He's mad about her and has asked her to come and live with him. The trouble is, she's got a sister – an identical twin. Now he doesn't know which twin he's asked. 'I fink I've 'ad 'em both, see.'

Now he's gone off filming, praying the problem will sort itself out.

I promised you news of Attila the Gun. The first bulletin came from my distressed son at school. 'He's laid up, mum; injured.' Attila, as you know, is Clive's hero. He's forever skipping classes and rehearsals to go and watch him massacre the opposition at cricket. Now he's out of the game for at least a month, and Clive's distraught. So is Lottie, who brought me the second bulletin. Apparently Attila put his hip out practising something unorthodox with her in the bedroom; she wouldn't say what. The papers say he injured himself 'during a training session', which is one way of putting it. A further domestic complication at No 9 is the likely return of husband Maurice the ad-man from foreign parts. Little does he know that foreign parts have already taken possession at home.

It should be interesting, and I will report.

Clive's recital at the Wigmore Hall is the week after next. He played me the Bartok sonata at the weekend. I was bursting with pride and enquired how he could possibly read music so fast. 'I don't,' he said. And when I leant over, the score in front of him turned out to be a girlie magazine. The wretch had learnt the piece by heart.

I confess a photo of you greeting the Prime Minister on all fours even made the front page of *The Independent*. I did think at first that you seemed to be taking your duties as First Lady a bit too seriously. Then I read on, and wept for you. Tom, as you know, believes health to be a highly dangerous thing. I'm afraid you may have proved his point. He shook his head and looked sad. 'Such a wonderful woman,' he said. 'And what about me?' I chipped in. 'Yeah, you're all right,' he added charmingly. That set back the day when he can screw me for several months, I can tell you.

Has this letter cheered you up a little? I should like to think so.

Ah, Ambrose has just walked past, peering foxily through the window. If he's long-sighted he'll have seen Prawns *Soixante-Neuf*, though I doubt if No 69 means anything more to him than the address of the Savile Club in Brook Street, to which he once invited me for 'luncheon', as he put it.

With very great love,

Janice.

British Embassy
Madrid

May 26th

Dear Harry,

No, I attended mercifully little of the E.C. conference, thanks largely to Ruth's much-publicised performance as a quadruped. I was excused on 'nursing leave', and the new First Secretary took over my duties as sycophant. He informs me the PM radiated goodwill and self-importance, again thanks to Ruth. Her airport collapse brought him front-page coverage throughout Europe and North America; so the world now actually knows who the new British Prime Minister is – something the government had failed to achieve ever since he took office. My wife certainly understands a thing or two about Public Relations.

She is better, I'm happy to say, though still confined to barracks. She walks with difficulty, and is visited daily by a muscle-bound harpy who kneads her like dough and demands large quantities of same after each session. Thank heaven for BUPA.

Otherwise she reads. For obvious reasons the British Council library is ruled out as a source of supply, so her literature is restricted to the motley collection we have in the flat. Teresa, our maid, nobly volunteers to stay behind and prepare dinner, so things are definitely looking up in that direction. My indigestion is now under control at least.

I get the feeling you may be confusing El Greco with some other painter. When I compared Angelica to an El Greco madonna I was not trying to imply that I was the angel of the Annunciation, nor that I was preparing myself for an Immaculate Conception – though immaculate it would have to be. I never quite understand the Roman Catholic insistence on virginity, though in Angelica's case I deeply respect it. She is in fact a profoundly religious person, and has recently taken to attending Sunday mass with a group of young Spaniards. I'm glad that in a foreign country she is beginning to make friends with some of the locals: it makes me feel better about not being with her as often as I should like.

Unfortunately I've had to postpone the visit to Toledo until next month. Angelica is disappointed but very patient. She is looking radiant and lovelier than ever.

I hear rumbles from London that a permanent Head of Mission may be arriving before the autumn, and that I may be borne on the wings of a dove to become ambassador, possibly to one of the newly-recognised nations. I rack my brains anxiously. The Baltic States? Slovenia? Armenia? Or, knowing my luck, some leech-infested islet in the Pacific whose aboriginal inhabitants still progress on all fours, and will no doubt elect Ruth as their queen unless her present condition improves.

It was sad news that you and Janice now have your decree *nisi.* I always hoped you'd both of you pull back from the brink. She remains one of the most beautiful creatures I know. It'll be a lucky man who gets her. Ruth is convinced she'll never marry again; and I suppose after you this might not be entirely surprising.

All the best,
Piers.

June

93 Avenida de Cervantes
Madrid

June 2nd

Dear Janice,

This may be a long letter since I'm still partially laid up and have fuck-all else to do except read, which I've been doing extensively. I don't think the Conway library would qualify as an Important National Treasure, or that the government would accept it in lieu of death duties along with Piers' reproduction of Renoir's *Les Parapluies* and the palette-knife harbour scenes at sunset presented to him by the grateful Malaysians. I suppose my mother's *Yom Kippur in Nazareth* might be snapped up by an old people's home in Bethnal Green, but that's about the long and the short of it. Piers may be cultured to the eyeballs but it doesn't extend to the home environment. And I have no culture at all.

So I've been reading whatever comes to hand, dictated by chance and circumstance. It began with circumstance. Piers, having nannied me for a week, slithered out to have dinner with tweetie-pie. I was stuck here raging and miserable. I'd seen nothing except the view of the house opposite for seven days. At eight o'clock punctually every morning a crone hangs her knickers out of the window to dry (whatever does she do to them all night?), where they billow like a spinnaker in the Fastnet race until they take on exactly the shape they must be when she's wearing them. This is not the way I would choose my days to begin. Neither is Piers cocooned elsewhere with his mistress how I would choose them to end.

It was late. But I wasn't tired. I decided to read. Do you remember that book you gave me when you were separated from Harry the first time? You were discovering Women's Lib rather late in life, you said, and wanted to share the experience with me. Well, I *didn't* want to share it then because I felt entirely liberated as it was, and couldn't stand the idea of some Harvard amazon ordering me to glory in my bodily functions and throw all my make-up in the trash can. So I never read it.

But that night I did. I wanted to receive the message. I wanted to stand on the feminist barricades. I wanted to be told that men were a load of shit.

Most of all I wanted to be told that we women could do without them – that a woman's world could be complete and rich and fulfilling. That even sex could be more fulfilling without their horrible little willies with such huge and fragile egos in tow; willies that would never stand up when you wanted them to, or came at you rampant when you didn't want them to, or exploded too soon or else long after you wished they'd wither away. Why not dildoes, vibrators, French ticklers – the lot?: they were at our command, whatever shape, size, performance we might wish, and for as long and whenever we wished. It all sounded great. I prepared myself for an experience that would make Piers bonking tweetie-pie an event entirely irrelevant to my life: as far as I was concerned he could stay out as many nights as he liked, screw whoever he liked, swing from chandeliers, do it in the shower, on the ironing-board, in the embassy loo, in a restaurant between the *gazpacho* and the *cordero lechal asado*, on the library shelves among old bound volumes of *The Illustrated London News*, or roped on a high mountain ledge like his athletic predecessor. And I wouldn't care. I was my own master and mistress. What he chose to do with his all-conquering member was no concern of mine whatsoever.

So I settled down to read your book. Or, rather, I tried to read your book. And sure enough it did manage to say most of the things I expected it to say. The trouble was, coming from your Harvard amazon it all sounded quite different. It began to annoy me. I found myself saying, 'What a lot of crap', 'You silly cow', 'This is not me at all', 'You seem to have missed the whole point of what life is about'.

I put the book down in tears. All I could think of was that Piers was with another woman, not me. That was what mattered in my life. I was so jealous I hurled the book across the room.

Anger always came to my rescue. And after anger, bloody-mindedness. A mail order catalogue had come through the post that morning – *The International Buyers Guide*. How did they know me or my address so quickly? I feel followed by invisible eyes. I don't even know why I decided to open it – I normally don't. 'A warm welcome to our latest review of brand-new products,' it announced.

The woman who said it was smiling. I scowled at her; then I started turning the pages. I became intrigued by the extraordinary things I was supposed to find indispensable to my life. An '*improved* trouser press', 'scissors tough enough to cut money', 'Sonic Super Ears', 'world's first automatic scrubbing-brush', 'ultrasonic pet collar'.

Having decided that Piers could probably survive without these, I was about to chuck the catalogue in the bin when something caught my eye. 'The most versatile tool ever.' Now, how about that for Piers? The text was even better. 'This magic tube is all you need to transfer liquids without mess or having to suck to start the flow.' Well, I thought; how simply wonderful. I marked the page and went on turning. Soon there appeared another 'must' for my husband. 'Rapid Inflation – the integral gauge will tell you when you've got the right pressure.' Now that surely would make tweetie-pie's life a lot more comfortable, wouldn't it? The right pressure: every girl wants that. Save Piers a lot of trouble. And then another! 'Goo Gone solves every sticky problem.' Just in case the 'versatile tool' should get the 'right pressure' rather unexpectedly, I suppose. I could already hear tweetie-pie gasping, 'It's all right, darling, it's quite Goo Gone. Nightie-night.'

By now I was in an absolutely terrific mood. If it hadn't been past midnight I'd have picked up the phone and got straight on to the Priority Orderline – 'I'd like the following items posted immediately to the British Embassy in Madrid, please. The name's Conway. No address necessary: everybody knows the Chargé d'Affaires. Here's his Access number . . .'

I fell asleep instead. And in the morning I didn't feel like it. I don't know what time Piers came in: I could hear no sound from his room. The silence of guilt and satiety.

Teresa found me crying over breakfast.

You used to tell me how children bounce: laughter one minute, tears the next. In that case there's a child in every unhappy wife. I often don't know what I am any more: moods overtake me like summer storms. Even when I'm writing to you, like now, depression hits me and I try to write through it, keep going till it passes. Or I reach for my sense of humour like lost spectacles. Coffee helps now that I'm off that disgusting healthy de-caff. In fact life is made extremely tolerable with the aid of stimulants to get me through the day, and alcohol in the evening as a reward for having made it thus far. Fund-raising suffers, but I survive.

What self-pity all this is. Let me tell you about my further reading instead.

After breakfast I managed a smile for Piers as he left for the embassy – 'Yes, my back feels better, thank you' – and then I gazed idly at the bookshelves again. They seemed like a memento of all those empty hours at airports buying novels you don't want and waiting for planes that don't arrive – Athens flight: Due 09.30, Expected 14.15 . . . Air traffic control over France (the bloody frogs) . . . Ding dong: 'Will Mrs Conway kindly report to the Information Desk,' Shit! After all that I've missed him, or else he's not even on the fucking plane.

My eye came to rest on a black book with silver lettering: Lyndoe's *Plan with the Planets.* Plan what with the planets? The question was intriguing enough to make me reach out – ouch, my back! – and open it. The author, I read, had been 'Astrological adviser to *The People* newspaper continuously since 1933.' Christ, he must be as old as the stars himself, I thought. Then I saw that the book was published by Herbert Jenkins in 1949: I suppose Piers must have picked it up in a jumble sale. Well, the planets don't exactly date, do they? So I started to read it.

I've always maintained I never believe a word of any horoscope, and then of course I read them carefully. The introduction caught my eye. It listed lots of things the author was certain I would wish to know, the last one being 'How you stand in regard to marriage'. Yes, I would like to know how I stand in regard to my marriage. Wobbly, in my view. To find out, the book said, I needed first of all to know my star sign. So I checked it out. Apparently I'm Sagittarius. 'Sagittarians,' it said, 'have a healthy outlook on the subject of sex.' Well, that was a good beginning. Encouraged, I read on. 'Most of them pass through a wayward phase (Yes, I could be said to have done that), but few fail to settle down to a predominant attachment (Yup!). They are high-powered people who often endure needless misery (Absolutely) because of their light-hearted, experimental approach to love.' (Now, wait a minute, he's got it wrong there: I was *broken*-hearted, not light-hearted. And experimental? It's true I've done quite a bit of experimenting, especially with the French Ambassador in Athens; but how else are you supposed to find out what you like?) I remembered the book was written a long time ago, and decided Mr Lyndoe was probably rather old-fashioned in these matters: the missionary position with the lights off and pyjamas on.

But in general this was all rather encouraging. The book said a bit more about me under the section 'Worries'. 'Favourite worries: dispute or misunderstandings caused by tactless or emotional moves.' And what was I to do about them? 'Your main danger lies in hiding your worry or attempting some deception to avoid the consequences. Frankness is your great asset. Be candid and open; meet the trouble if it has to come.'

By now I was hooked. Mr Lyndoe, whether you're still with us or up there among your stars, you are my man. So I was a Sagittarian. That was fascinating. It was like suddenly having a family I'd never known about.

This made me wonder who else belonged to my remarkable family, and what I might have in common with them. I turned to the section entitled *Celebrated Sagittarians.* At first there seemed to be a disappointing number of nonentities: but then – pow! Winston Churchill. Mary Queen of Scots. Nostradamus. Milton. Beethoven. Ralph Richardson. *And* Ruth Conway!

It was a bit early in the day but I felt I deserved a drink for being in such exalted company. Teresa looked surprised but seemed to think it was medicinal and helped me back to my chair with a comforting smile.

The next task was clearly Piers. What star sign might he be? Aries, I discovered. Now, this was going to be really interesting. *Your Love Life. Aries.* 'A great deal of inner warfare is generated by sexual questions.' (Ah ha! Inner warfare, eh!) 'He likes to feel he has control of himself and of his destiny. Often he fails.' (Got him. Fail he will.) Next I turned to an Arian's habits and worries: they all seemed extremely boring; but then Piers' habits and worries are extremely boring. Mr Lyndoe had got it right again. I moved on to *An Aries Digest.* 'The sign for Aries is the heavenly ram' (Spot on, matey: tweetie-pie would know all about that, the bitch). 'Favourite stone is the diamond.' (He'd better not give her too many of those or he'll be in deep trouble.) 'Stimulants are not recommended to Arians except in small quantities.' (I wonder what the author means by 'stimulants'. Coffee or assistant librarians? But I like the 'small quantities' bit: perhaps 'none at all' would be even more strongly recommended.) And what about Piers' newly-discovered family? I turned to *Celebrated Arians.* The first name to catch my eye was Joseph Ignace Guillotin, inventor. The next was King Richard II of England. (One executioner, one executed: Piers isn't doing too well.) The list looked up slightly after that. Paul Robeson, singer. John Jackson, celebrated divine. Pierre Laplace, French savant (Who he? - Ed). William Harvey, discoverer of blood circulation. Admiral the Viscount Exmouth. Definitely a second-rate family all in all. What a good thing he married into mine, I decided.

The question was – how to keep it that way?

Janice, I'm a fanciful woman. I yield to impulses. I leap, often forgetting my safety harness. I've done many foolish things trying to rid my life of tweetie-pie, and sometimes I think it's the shock of what Piers has done that has caused me to act as I have. Too often I've behaved like a scalded puppy.

I must put a stop to all that. Mr Lyndoe's book may be a load of codswallop for all I know, but it has suggested to me something valuable – the need to understand who

I am, who my partner is, and why therefore we do the things we do.

I closed the little black book feeling very calm and in command. I resolved that hereafter I would be magnificently mature, regally lofty and wise, and that I would treat the aberrations of my Arian husband as mere peccadilloes no more damaging to our marriage than a bout of hay-fever, or in his case an attack of piles (which are worse – hee! hee!).

I even turned the page of my sun-tan calendar to see in what fresh guise tweetie-pie might confront me for the month of June. She is – I'm delighted to say – quite the silliest yet. She has a smile which exactly imitates the radiator grille of an Oldsmobile I once crashed in New Mexico, and nipples that remind me of those rubber suction-gadgets that are so useful for unblocking the sink.

And now Ruth Conway intends to rise from her bed and walk. I can bear to contemplate my neighbour's knickers no longer. I shall take my Sagittarian self slowly and majestically to the Retiro Gardens; and after that to the Prado where, with a thought for you in River Mews, I shall identify with the sophistication of Titian's reclining ladies, making sure I post this on the way,

bearing much love and best wishes
for all your naughty dishes,
Ruth Revived.

Palacio Pizarro
Trujillo

June 5th

Dear Ruth Conway,

I have no personal experience of an 'exercise machine', though I recall some years ago staying with an American president, I forget which, who employed something similar on account of his back. There was no evidence that it improved his condition, though I formed the opinion that his extra-presidential activities nullified any beneficial effects it may have had. I always intended to point out this contradiction to him, but he was assassinated before I had the opportunity. A kind man.

It was a relief to hear that the wine reached you in good condition. I was uneasy about using the royal carrier in case the pilot confused its destination, but conventional methods of transport are so unreliable in this country, and a helicopter was at least quick and likely to cause less disturbance to the wine. I am glad I insisted that Xavier have a flight-roof incorporated into the design of the hospital – as you know, he owns it. I fear the new chef leaves something to be desired: his predecessor found the offer from Maxim's irresistible. Did you find the *cuisine* intolerable?

No, I have no more experience of astrology than of exercise machines. It strikes me as most unlikely that my own fortunes are guided by some conjunction of remote constellations. Anyone who gazed at the heavens at the moment of my birth – and I'm told many did - would have witnessed twinkles which took place a great many billions of years before I was even a twinkle in my father's eye. This simple scientific fact would seem to me the principal flaw in astrologists' thinking, if indeed they may be said to think at all.

My own stars, as it were, have improved with the return of Luis from his honeymoon. He looks most unwell, poor lad: it has been quite an ordeal. But I reassure him that this being a Catholic country of a conventional kind, it is unlikely to happen again. He was cheered by this, and happily his strength returns daily now he has resumed his normal duties. Miguel was unsatisfactory in this respect and has departed to the family smallholding.

Please grant me your excellent company just as soon as you are well. The weather here is delightful, and it is the apricot season.

With best wishes,

Estelle.

16c Iffley Street
London W6

June 7th

Dear Nauti-less,

My tearful condolences to you for being flat on your back, though the position can't be altogether unfamiliar.

Any tetchiness in the tone of this letter is due to the attentions of one of my former wives, Georgina, whose mid-life crisis is taking the form of believing her house to be haunted. Ghosts I can deal with, and have written a number of newspaper stories about them. But this one happens to be Emily Bronte. My ex-wife is convinced Ms Bronte is dictating her a novel. And not just a novel but the sequel to *Wuthering Heights* which death prevented her from writing herself. She insists (my ex-wife, that is, not Emily Bronte) that I be the lady's amanuensis since I know shorthand and she doesn't.

The absurdity of this situation will not have escaped you. I have never read *Wuthering Heights.* In fact I have hardly read anything in my life: I was always too busy getting divorced. And can you imagine me taking dictation from a ghost? Georgina rings constantly to stress the urgency. I stall by pointing out that since Ms Bronte has already been dead one-and-a-half centuries the novel is unlikely to run away. She rings again adamant that the creative moment is the creative moment, and must be seized. I only wish the men in white coats would seize *her*. Then she rings yet again screaming that the first chapter is already lost to posterity. Once I agreed to go round to the house with my shorthand notebook – a journalist never lets slip the smallest chance of a story. The ghost never appeared. Georgina claimed it was because I wasn't in a receptive mood. This was perfectly true. So I went home. An hour later she rang again saying Emily Bronte was waiting. I'm afraid I suggested Ms Bronte learn to use a word-processor. Georgina slammed down the phone.

All this may sound amusing to you reclining on your sick bed. But these phone calls invariably come when I have a deadline to meet for the paper, or when Janice is showing every sign of abandoning herself to my charms. It's no use my telling the editor, or Janice, that I've been unavoidably distracted by the ghost of Emily Bronte. The editor threatens to fire me, and Janice is convinced I'm up to no good with another woman.

She meanwhile produces illustrations for *Prawnography* which delight the publisher and fire me with lustful anticipation of our future life together if Janice will have me. But until I can lay the ghost I can hardly expect to lay her, let alone propose marriage.

Can I send you anything? Can I do anything for you? How about a copy of *Wuthering Heights* Part Two signed by the author?

For the moment, awaiting your command, I'll just send you my love,

Tom.

93 Avenida de Cervantes
Madrid

June 12th

Dear Janice,

Marital Repairs Service Report No 4

Thirty-one days to Waterloo, and campaign strategy is changing.

Let me begin quietly. My recovery after consulting the stars was miraculous: if God sits up there no wonder people pray to him. What I've missed out on all these years – a heavenly NHS.

I posted my last letter on my way to the Retiro Gardens and the Prado: my first outing for well over a week. It's extraordinary how vulnerable one feels. I flattened myself against a wall every time a car passed. Crossing the road was like the Battle of the Somme. I slumped into a pavement café and shook. The dual-carriageway opposite the Prado was quite beyond me. I stood quivering by the kerb until an American couple took pity on me. I lied that I'd just come out of hospital and they guided me across, comforting me with their name, address and an account of their daughter's miscarriage. I needed to sit down again before I could tackle Titian.

Now, you are an arty person and steeped in these things, whereas I've never managed to experience anything much in the presence of great art beyond the sensation of feeling worthily bored. Pictures act on me rather like valium: they calm the nerves and make me dopey. I wander woozily around feeling reassured by all those famous names and far-fetched images until I've done it long enough to deserve a stiff drink. After several drinks I become convinced I've had a wonderfully uplifting time, though actually I don't believe I've taken the pictures in at all. I know they're important, so they become important to me. On the whole I greatly prefer ruins, where it's only the wandering that matters. You aren't expected to *look* at ruins, or be uplifted by them: they're just there, and the odd Corinthian column left standing makes a stunning foreground to the view, and invites you to photograph it.

If they were all standing you wouldn't be able to see the view at all, and if none of them were it would be thoroughly ordinary and you wouldn't even notice it. This seems to me the secret of ruins. Besides they don't spray them with insecticides, so there are always flowers, lizards, butterflies and things; and because tourists are forever eating there are interesting birds who come for the crumbs. You also meet fascinating people at ruins, which you don't in museums – romantic people who, like me, are taking their daydreams for a walk. I've had some of the most interesting conversations of my life in ruins, and met quite a few of my lovers. When I shared this information with Estelle she imagined I abandoned myself on the spot and said, 'Really, my dear, isn't it rather uncomfortable on a Roman drainage system?'

I'm not sure why I'm telling you all this; perhaps it's the sheer joy of belonging to the human race once again. I'm also about to surprise you with the news that I'm not quite as philistine as I seem. I went to the Prado to find a woman I could identify with in my new super-cool Sagittarian mode. I thought Titian might deliver the goods, and indeed he did. You undoubtedly know the picture well. It's a bacchanalia. Just about everything is going on, aided by a great deal of wine and hopping about with bare thighs and arms whirling, not unlike those desperate parties in Los Angeles which Piers used to pretend he hated.

But, there in the foreground of all these shinnanagins was this cool, detached creature reclining in the sun – not dissimilar to me in shape, although blonde, with smaller tits and no pubic hair. Apart from a mischievous urchin close by who looked as if he might pee on her any minute, here was my ideal Sagittarian role model: she was exactly the woman I needed to be in the present circumstances, a beautiful unruffled presence amid an orgy of drunken lechery.

I also made an important discovery which may surprise scholars – that great art needs to be about *me*. If I can't identify, sod it.

For a long time I continued to gaze at the picture. Yes, there was the Angelica figure flashing her thighs in a wanton fashion, and Piers ogling her *décolletage* and looking a bit thin on top. Substitute a diplomat's suit for the man's red robe, and clingfilm jeans for her flimsies, and real life was all there. And the lady, my *alter ego*, remained quite unaffected, undeterred; she was the one who had seen it all before, these childish games; she had finer things on her mind. That was me.

The sun was shining outside the Prado. I sipped a *limon granizado* in an open-air café. The summer was warming up, and life felt good. I thanked Mr Lyndoe for his 'plan with the planets', and I thanked Titian for showing me myself. It no longer mattered what Piers and tweetie-pie got up to: it was just one of those foolish things. We Sagittarians, I remembered, were 'sufficiently buoyant to take all obstacles in their stride', in Lyndoe's words.

Back at the flat I found Piers had returned early from the embassy. This is not unusual: he takes the view that if he doesn't show up, no work will either. But now he seemed restless, as though he'd been waiting for me; whenever there's something on Piers' mind it shines out like a beacon. Since anything on Piers' mind at the moment tends to be unwelcome to my ears, I said nothing and unfolded a reproduction of the Titian I'd bought in the museum bookshop. He didn't even glance at it, in spite of the nudes.

I just waited for him to say something.

'By the way, I'm thinking of taking some of the weekend off,' he announced airily after several minutes of pounding about.

Now, Piers normally takes the entire weekend off like everyone else at the embassy; so what was he getting at?

'I see,' I said, keeping extremely cool. 'Anything special?'

'Oh, not really,' he went on a little too hastily. 'I thought I'd like to get out of Madrid for a while.'

I kept up my Sagittarian calm.

'I'm sure that's a good idea, darling. Anywhere in particular?'

There was a slight pause.

'It occurred to me Toledo wasn't too far.'

'Oh, indeed! Lovely place,' I said. 'I remember admiring the El Grecos there with you once.' My God, I was doing well. Piers was clearly encouraged. 'And as you say,' I went on, 'it's not at all far: you can be back in an hour or so.'

That made him look a little awkward. There was a pause and a cough. He examined his knuckles.

'Well of course, there *is* so much to see it might be better if I spent a night there.'

Ah ha! It was rather like watching a rabbit emerging from its burrow.

'Oh, I'm sure that's right,' I said reassuringly. 'Then

you can get to that wonderful cathedral early before the tourists arrive, can't you?' Piers was trying to look as though nothing could possibly be more delightful than looking at a wonderful cathedral in the early morning. 'And since you're back so early,' I went on, smiling, 'you could even go today, couldn't you?' His face brightened cautiously. 'And then you could have two nights in Toledo if you wanted,' I suggested.

The head was nodding gravely. All these unexpected goodies coming his way, he must have thought it was Christmas.

'Yes, I could; I certainly could.'

'And in that case you could spend lots and lots of time in front of the El Grecos, and enjoy the cathedral in all its different magic moments.'

I wasn't quite sure if he thought I was taking the piss or not. I also wasn't sure if he was waiting for me to say, 'Look, you lying creep, why don't you just say you want to fuck your little tart morning, noon and night?' I'm sure he would have been prepared for that, and given me one of his homilies about spiritual love. As it was, he didn't need to. Sagittarian Ruth was behaving quite immaculately.

I kept it up until he'd packed his bag and slipped out of the flat looking awkwardly pleased with himself. I stood by the window for a while, gazing at the dismal street; then at our own dreadful pictures on the wall, at the sun-tan girl with the rubber-suction nipples, and finally at our unloved bookshelves where Lyndoe's *Plan with the Planets* now leaned against something unread from a Booker shortlist several years ago.

I picked up Mr Lyndoe's little black book. 'Thank

you, kind sir,' I said aloud. 'You have taught me my true nature as a Sagittarian so perfectly that I have just sent my husband off to screw his bimbo for two nights with all the love and blessing with which my star-sign endowed me.'

And I chucked the book across the room, flung open the window, and yelled after my long-departed husband – "You fucking arsehole!"

End of Marital Repairs Service Report. And end of planning with the planets.

I'm not sure where I went, but Madrid seemed to be moving round me like jostling ghosts. I kept saying to myself, 'This is the end; this is the end.' It nearly was *my* end as I did the English thing and looked right instead of left crossing the Gran Via. In my best Spanish I called the startled driver a fascist pig and promptly walked straight into a barrow piled with aubergines. Then I collapsed into a café in the Plaza Mayor and couldn't see my coffee for tears. I felt too upset to care that people kept coming up and asking if I was all right. 'No, I'm not,' I answered, and they went away. I remember thinking, 'Why do they bother to ask?'

Then a priest took my hand and called me 'my child', which was strangely comforting. I told him my story between gurgles and sobs, and he said, 'Do you love him a great deal?' I told him, 'Yes, and he's an absolute shit.' To my slight indignation he laughed. I was a woman of great fortitude, he said – '*Firmeza, firmeza.*' He repeated the word several times, thumping my hand on the table. I don't know the Spanish for 'Well, that's fuck-all use to me, is it?' but I managed some sort of equivalent, whereupon he laughed again and gave my hand another thump. 'What I suggest,' he went on, 'is that you make him jealous. Find another man.' I gazed at him in astonishment through my tears. 'You're supposed to be a priest,' I said indignantly. His face broke into a grin. 'I'm supposed to be, but I'm not,' he answered. 'I'm an actor.' And at that moment I heard voices raised across the square. I looked up, and there fifty yards away a Spanish television crew were setting up cameras and lights. The director was shouting, 'Sancho, we're ready.' Sancho got up, then leant over and kissed my hand. 'I meant it, señora. *Firmeza. Firmeza.* You're also beautiful.' He stood up and looked very serious: he was a handsome man. 'I'd offer to make your husband jealous for you,' he said, 'but I'm homosexual.'

He gave me a kiss on the cheek and hurried away.

I stayed out late that evening: I couldn't bear to return to the flat. I thought of checking into a hotel, but I had no money, no credit cards, nothing. And would it have been any better? Hotels are lonely places. If only I had a real home, I thought. Diplomats live borrowed lives in borrowed houses: wives are part of the baggage-train.

When I finally got back the flat was in darkness. At least there was no grovelling note from Piers on my pillow telling me he loved me really. In a burst of anger I wrenched all his clothes out of the cupboard, shoved them into a suitcase and left it outside the door. Half an hour later the doorbell rang and the lady opposite sweetly pointed to the suitcase and said, 'I think that must be for you.' I'd forgotten the case had 'Piers Conway' inscribed on it. I put all the clothes carefully back. Then I had a fit of creativity and composed a wonderfully disgusting limerick which I decided to cable him in the morning if I could discover where he was staying. That blunted my misery for a short while – but I couldn't sleep.

Janice, is there any pain quite like sexual jealousy? He'd be in bed with her now, I kept thinking. There'd be the same moon I could see, the same stars, the same warm night. I could hardly bear to think of them, wherever they were – two bodies, one I knew, one I didn't, one I loved, one I hated. There was a cruel touch too – something I never knew about – how erotic it was imagining them together, what they were doing, where he was touching her, she him, the sounds, the breathing, he discovering her, she discovering the things I knew so well.

Then there was the remorse. Would it have happened if I'd always been faithful? Was this my punishment?

It was five in the morning and the faintest of dawns, so perhaps I had slept an hour or two without knowing. I found myself repeating '*Firmeza, firmeza.*' The thought of the homosexual actor-priest even managed to make me laugh. *Firmeza. Firmeza.* Yes, I needed to be that, didn't I? I made myself some coffee and watched the morning spread over the houses opposite. Oh God, I thought, any minute the knickers are going to appear.

I had a bath, changed my clothes and made myself eat some cornflakes. That, I said to myself, was the worst night of my life.

I wasn't greatly looking forward to the day either, and was wondering what the hell to do with it when the phone rang. My first thought was, 'It's Piers telling me he's never coming back.' My second thought was, 'It's Piers telling me he *is* coming back.' By the time I actually picked up the receiver I was in a state of confusion and could hardly say 'Hello'.

It was Esteban. He sounded excited. We'd pulled off a coup, he said. The finest collection of Inca gold in Spain had been offered as a gift to the Museum of the Conquistadors in Trujillo, and would become the focus of the exhibition in London. 'It's entirely due to you, *señora*,' he kept saying. 'You have triumphed.'

He then mentioned a name which rang a bell. 'You had lunch with him the day before your accident – remember?' I sort of remembered: there had been a monotony of fundraising lunches recently with grey men who looked and talked alike, and I've never been good at names. Most of the time I had no idea who they were: Xavier or Esteban produced them on a conveyor-belt, and they either did or did not pay up, and either did or did not invite me to bed.

'He was the one you referred to as Don Juan Halitosis,' Esteban reminded me.

Now I remembered clearly.

'Well, he said you were his Queen of Heaven, and you could have whatever you asked. What *did* you ask, *señora*?'

The truth is I had no idea. I have a choice of several prepared spiels for these lechers I wine and dine, depending on whether they are industrialists, bankers or serious collectors. I either make a polite request for money, or a loan of something, and I invariably preface it with 'in the interests of our two historic nations . . .' and all that crap.

Blowing the dust off my memory of Don Juan Halitosis I recall being convinced he was a prominent banker and therefore suggesting *una donación*. It's also true that I remember him looking a trifle startled and then placing his hand on my knee. No cheque was forthcoming, which I attributed to the speed with which I removed his hand and recoiled from his breath.

But according to Esteban, who was present at the time, it appears that I requested his entire collection as a *donación*. My Spanish is presumably to blame for this; but in any case we've now got it. Instead of a cheque for 50,000 pesetas I've apparently acquired half the gold of El Dorado. Estelle will be proud of me.

'Please let us celebrate at my hacienda,' Esteban was saying. 'I would be honoured.'

But I wasn't listening. An idea had come to me – a brilliant idea. And as soon as I'd got rid of Esteban I telephoned Tom. (This bit you undoubtedly know, but let me give you my angle.) I'm afraid Tom was probably asleep: I'd forgotten Spanish clocks are an hour ahead. His voice came to me through gravel. But journalists are like cats, aren't they? If they sleep too deeply the story may sneak away in the dark.

'Tom, I've got an exclusive for you,' I announced. 'Are you ready?'

I then told him. I also explained there was a condition attached. However he might choose to write the story, he absolutely had to make a banquet of the diplomatic acumen, social triumphs, incandescent beauty and generally irresistible personality of Her Majesty's First Lady in Madrid: 'cementing relations between our countries', 'smoothing over the ugly business of Gibraltar', 'bringing the latest London fashions into the heart of Madrid society', 'the brightest jewel in Britain's crown is at present . . .'. All that sort of thing, and more, I said to Tom. There was a grunt, then a pause. For an embarrassing moment I wondered if perhaps you were lying next to him, or under him.

'OK, doll; I'll give it a whirl,' he said grumpily. 'Do you mind if I wake up first?'

So that was it. I made Tom take down the basic information he needed, then a few facts about the conquistadors' museum and the London exhibition, plus the names of some useful contacts, Xavier, Estelle, etc. 'You certainly know how to deal with hangovers,' Tom said.

Now I await results. Is Ruth Conway about to hit the tabloids? And what will our sophisticated Chargé d'Affaires feel when forced to compare his glittering wife with the timid little library assistant he was once foolish enough to eye?

Anyway, I was elated. It's goodbye Sagittarius: I'm about to become a *real* star.

And then a further thought came to me. Since I was about to enjoy the fruits of personal triumph, why not have one for real? So I rang Esteban and accepted his invitation to the hacienda. After all, it was only what the actor-priest suggested. And with his public school sense of fair play Piers is unlikely to object. One good weekend deserves another, wouldn't you agree?

It won't be for another couple of weeks. That will give Piers plenty of time to look forward to it.

Got any good recipes I can take with me? How about Spanish Cocktail with Undressed Prawns?

All love,

Ruth.

British Embassy
Madrid

June 15th

Dear Harry,

Yes, the weekend in Toledo was a success, though not in the manner you tastelessly suggest in your letter. In fact we spent very little time in bed, and in any case took separate rooms. We rose early each morning to explore the city before the heat, and Angelica was particularly thrilled by the cathedral – superb stained-glass – and of course the El Grecos. By the late afternoon we were both of us grateful for the hotel pool. Angelica's bathing-costume, I have to say, was not what you might have expected from someone who'd been lighting a candle to St Ildefonsus only an hour or two earlier, though it was modesty itself compared to several of the Germans who seemed to think this was the Costa del Sol. I'd often wondered where German women put all those cakes.

The only dark cloud hanging over an otherwise delightful weekend was the behaviour of Ruth, who persists in believing – as you so delicately put it yourself – that I am 'getting it up every five minutes'. Platonic love is something she simply doesn't understand, presumably never having known it, and a deaf ear is turned to whatever I say on the subject. At our breakfast table in Toledo a cable awaited me consisting of one of her more inventive limericks, which would have been deeply offensive to Angelica had I not swiftly hidden it under a bread roll; though in fact I very much doubt if the girl would have known what some of the words meant. I find it miraculous how beauty can enshrine a certain innocence in some people – not an observation I have ever felt tempted to make about you, I may say.

I'm sorry the senator returned at the wrong moment. You are fortunate he is so rarely sober. Certainly in Madrid he never was.

Ruth has done wonders raising support for the museum of Red Indian loot she is involved in for some reason. If you see the odd second-hand tomahawk on your travels, kindly send it, though not personally to her or she may prefer to use it on me in her present mood. She is taking a weekend in the country shortly, she announced today. After the misery of her back, proper exercise and country air will do her the world of good.

The Prime Minister intends to holiday here during the summer recess, so I'm informed by No 10. Perhaps he imagines he will make the front page of the world's press each time he comes to Spain. Someone needs to tell the vain little man that it was my wife in her canine role they were photographing last time. In any case most Spaniards still believe Mrs Thatcher is our PM, and speak of her with horrible affection. I await a shrine in the cathedral. St Ildefonsus may soon be eclipsed.

I hear your lovely 'ex' is about to make her fortune

on a cookery book. Perhaps she can be encouraged to wing a copy to Ruth. Josceline Dimbleby's *Marvellous Meals with Mince* has already enjoyed a fearfully long innings on our home ground.

Ours is the only embassy in Madrid not to have air-conditioning. The result is even more hot air than is usual in a foreign mission.

With best wishes.

Yours,

Piers.

MADRID 1000 HRS JUNE 16
CABLE DESPATCH TO: JANICE BLAKEMORE ONE
RIVER MEWS LONDON W4 UK READ INDEPENDENT NEWSPAPER SPECIALIST CONDOM SHOP SOHO STOP EXCITING BRANDS INCLUDE DUTCH STRAWBERRY FLAVOURED TUTTI FRUTTI PLUS GLOW IN DARK QUOTE NO MORE FUMBLE BEFORE YOU FONDLE UNQUOTE REQUEST URGENT EXPEDITION MY BEHALF SEND IN DIPLOMATIC BAG SIC
STOP FO ACCUSTOMED SUCH THINGS STOP HOORAY RUTH

1 River Mews

June 18th

Dearest Ruth,

I do hope my imaginative selection reaches you intact. The owner of the shop added one or two more on his personal recommendation, commenting breezily that since I was a lady he assumed they were for conventional use. I nodded coyly and explained they were for a friend. 'They all say that, darling,' he said. 'You've no need to be shy; we're very frank in the condom business.' Then I asked him if he'd mind wrapping them discreetly since they needed to travel by diplomatic bag. He laughed. 'Diplomatic bag, eh! We know all about them, darling. You should see the Arab diplomats who come in here: I ask them if they want the kind that points to Mecca. We even had the papal nuncio in last week – incognito of course, but I knew. Vatican men stick out a mile. Oops! Sorry! Excellent taste though, he had, I must say.' The man then produced a sort of sponge-bag with a crown printed on it in gold. 'We run a special diplomatic service, you see, darling. By royal appointment.' He laughed again. 'No trouble. Much appreciated in foreign parts, if you'll pardon the expression. Do come again. Oops! Sorry, darling. Have a good day – or night.'

It wasn't quite my usual kind of Saturday morning. Normally I'm in the deli, but Ching gave me the day off 'to do some shopping in the West End.'

Altogether it's been quite a week. On Monday Clive was expelled again, more or less on the anniversary of last time. I still don't quite believe all this. His recital at the Wigmore Hall was a resounding success, so I thought. I don't pretend to know the Bartok violin sonata well, but Clive seemed to me to be playing it brilliantly. I was aware of a certain undercurrent of noise from the audience towards the end, which I put down to bad manners. It wasn't until after it was over that the school head of music came up to me red-faced and spluttering. Apparently for the last part of the sonata Clive had substituted a piece 'of his own composing', as the man furiously put it to me.

And that was that. Out! End of scholarship. End of school. Clive, I have to say, remains quite unabashed. 'Fed up with the fucking fiddle,' he said. (His language is as bad as mine: I wonder where he gets it from.) 'I'm going to be a footballer.' Even cricket is forgotten now that Attila is laid up. And school? 'Wherever they play proper soccer; not that naff rugby stuff.' So he starts next week at the local comprehensive. All he asked was if there were girls there. Now I've got the little beast at home. He discovered my *Prawnography* illustrations yesterday and said, 'Ooh, Mum, how do you know about things like that?' Oh Jesus, I wish he'd go and live with his father.

The other major event of the week was the Creepy Crawleys' party at No 6. Mrs Creepy came into the deli and ordered a whole Brie, French bread, and lots of those Chinese polystyrene crisp things. As she left she confided – 'We're having a small gathering on Friday; I do hope you'll come.' She made it sound like a church service, and my spirits weren't exactly lifted by the sight of a bottle of Cyprus sherry peeping out of her shopping-bag. 'It's our house-warming,' she added confidentially. I knew the only warm thing would be the sherry, but I could hardly say 'No'. That evening I tried to ring Tom, then in desperation Kevin, who was just back from filming. 'For God's sake keep me company, Kev,' I pleaded, without mentioning the Cyprus sherry. 'You mean it's a piss-up?' he asked. I said I thought not exactly. 'Then I'd better get pissed first,' he said.

I turned up not quite impolitely late with the intention of leaving not quite impolitely early. Most of the street was already there. Nina was looking thunderously bored, and had parked her thimble of sherry on a church jumble sale notice where it was busy leaking a sticky brown ring. Lottie was doing her best to hide a love-bite on her neck the size of an orange, and Ah-man-dah all tits and chins was gazing up at Attila as if inviting the same, every so often glancing down between the bosoms at her empty thimble. The whole occasion was totally ghastly. Then to my relief I saw Kevin arrive a little unsteadily, grey hair dishevelled, one arm raised in greeting, the other round his Vietnamese beloved.

'This is Yin-and-Yang,' he announced to all and sundry; then to me more quietly – 'at least I think it is.' He's still not sure if he's got the right twin, or even the same twin as last time, so he avoids their names and refers to them collectively as Yin-and-Yang. 'I've decided t'be in love wiv 'em both, whichever one turns up,' he explained. 'What if both do, Kev?' I asked. He gave an explosive laugh. 'Then we'll 'ave a ball, won't we!' And he leaned forward and tapped my arm. 'I'n she lovely though?' His face was suddenly soft and tender. I gave him a kiss.

I was just preparing to slip away quietly when Mr

Creepy coughed significantly and called for silence. He began to make bright-eyed comments about how delighted he and his lady-wife were to be living in such a happy street, and proceeded to itemise the splendid qualities and achievements of his new neighbours as he saw them. It was exactly like an end-of-term speech. No one escaped the prize-giving. There was Kevin's contribution to the 'art of cinematography'. Then 'our healing friends' – that was Dr Angus and his wife. 'Our distinguished mediaevalist' (Roger of the birds). 'The spirit of Raphael reborn' (Ambrose Brown, R.A., painter of my nude portrait). 'King among sportsmen' (Attila the Gun). And so it went on. Thank God there are only ten houses in the street.

I was dreading my turn – and when it came it couldn't have been worse. Creepy had left me till last – deliberately, he explained, because he trusted that 'the enchanting Mrs Blakemore will now tell us about the exquisite illustrations she is making for the cookery book which I'm sure we are all impatient to acquire. It's title, Mrs Blakemore, is what exactly?'

They were all looking at me. Kindly expectant eyes – or at least most of them. The silence seemed eternal, the room a prison. I wanted to be sick, and the sherry didn't help. Then a miracle occurred. I hadn't seen Tom arrive. I'd left a panic message on his answering machine before I rang Kevin, but had heard nothing since and assumed he was away on a job.

At first I didn't even recognise his voice.

'As the author of the book perhaps I could speak for Janice who is modest about her own achievements.' Oh

God, I wanted to hug him. 'The book has no title as yet,' I heard Tom say smoothly, 'but it's to do with sea-food – recipes I've collected from many parts of the world. The illustrations I assure you are sublime. Mouth-watering, you might say.' There was polite laughter from the room. 'And now, if you'll excuse me, I'm going to take my co-author and collaborator out to dinner because although she doesn't know it we've just received an extremely handsome contract from America.'

I don't remember leaving. But I do remember dinner. It was a small French restaurant in Fulham. 'I've always wanted to bring you here,' Tom said. I wondered how many wives, how many other women, he'd brought before. And why now? For the first half of dinner I said to myself – 'No man has the right to be so charming: how I mistrust you.' For the second half I said to myself – 'I haven't been so happy for years: I want you, five times married or not. I want you to fuck me stupid.'

And he did.

Well, all I'm prepared to divulge at present is that he certainly makes love like a man who's had plenty of practice. He could have given me orgasms all night, the bastard. I had to leave much too early because of Clive, and as I staggered to my feet he laid his hands over my breasts and said, 'I love you.'

Ruth, I'm not sure what I am, what's going on, but whatever it is, I like it. It's been a long time. Are you happy for me? Your little Venus has come home.

With so much love,

Janice.

PS Tomorrow, to celebrate our celebration he's taking me to *Les Liaisons Dangereuses* at the RSC. Significant? His choice, not mine. Who's in danger, I wonder? The production, by the way, is about to tour, Tom says. First stop – Madrid. So, after your hacienda fiesta it might be exactly up your street. You must tell me all. And I'll tell you about Tom when I'm feeling less bashful. I feel very odd and can't stop smiling.

Palacio Pizarro
Trujillo

June 19th

Dear Ruth Conway,

Xavier is most contented with the Inca gold. I shall not enquire what you did to obtain it from Felipe. I once awarded him a similar favour in the interests of Children in Need, but that was a great many years ago. It was a small sacrifice for a million pounds, and I recall nothing of our union except a somewhat unpleasant odour which I'm told runs in the Bourbon family – no doubt too much inbreeding. The only other woman I know who welcomed his advances was Eva Peron, who usually possessed better taste though she may have been impecunious at the time: she *was* in exile. The sole comment Eva made to me was that Felipe's generosity was in inverse proportion to his size; and I hardly imagine he has grown much since. Men always worry themselves so much about these things. My first husband spent a fortune on oriental lotions during the few months we were together, but it would have taken a sharp eye to notice the difference, and my eye was already elsewhere.

But I digress. My warmest congratulations on your success. Thanks to you our modest little museum here in Trujillo will soon become a tourist honeypot, and there will be no peace for the wicked. I have asked Xavier to install double-glazing in the palace to muffle the sound of American voices. Luis nourishes ambitions to be the curator, but he rather confuses his qualifications, and I think I shall appoint someone from the Louvre. If only André Malraux were still alive: he would know just the man.

It is becoming unbearably hot. Take care when you stay with Esteban: his hacienda has little shade and he will certainly take you horse-riding. It is his passion, and he has a fine stable. The countryside there is glorious of course if you like that sort of thing. You will see many vultures. I know little of Esteban's own habits: his foolish fiancée is the last person to have any knowledge except of virginity, about which I am sure she is an expert (it's about the only subject Spanish women are allowed to become experts in). My daughter-in-law did enjoy a brief fête with him last year while my son was in jail, and acknowledged that he was ardent but unimaginative. He is of course extremely beautiful, which makes up for a lot when one grows bored.

All the same, now that you have decided to free yourself of fidelity I am confident we can soon find you someone more suitable than my rather ordinary nephew. I may enquire discreetly of Juan Carlos; he is certain to know – provided he has forgiven me for not selling him those vineyards. One always has to tread warily with royalty. With yours of course one treads warily because of the corgis.

I hope you will very soon honour me with another visit. We have much to celebrate, and we now have an excess of gold to drink from.

With my warmest wishes.

Yours,

Estelle.

16c Iffley Street
London W6

June 21st

Dear Ruth-amid-the-alien-Prawn,

Here's the article in the *Daily Scum* just in case the paper sold out in Madrid before you could lay your hands on it. We had some trouble with your photograph since the only one in our files showed you greeting the Prime Minister on all fours, which hardly supported the glamorous account I was writing. Fortunately Janice came to the rescue with one of you drinking champagne at last year's Wimbledon, which fitted the bill nicely, particularly since minor retouching by the art-room made you appear to be informing Princess Di of the finer points of tennis. My editor – who like all Scottish socialists is a raging snob – was specially impressed that your benefactor was a duke whose family had produced a dozen or more Spanish kings (hence of course the Inca gold). You never told me any of this on the phone: would I be right in thinking you didn't have the faintest idea who the man was? How very like you.

Anyway, I hope the piece has the desired effect, and Piers is at last valuing his pearl of great price. I need to make one apology. Being reticent by nature I took care to treat the subject of your physical charms most modestly, leaving much to the imagination; but I'm afraid by the time the subs finished with the article it did sound rather as though no more annihilating conquests had been witnessed in Spain since the Peninsula War. And for this I'm truly sorry: that's the tabloid press for you.

As a result I received a few phone-calls from gossip-hacks I do my very best to avoid. I put them off with a diversionary tactic – an entirely apocryphal story about the Primate of All Ireland which will fuel their loyalist sentiments and get them into a heap of trouble with the Press Council, not to mention the IRA.

Yes, Janice and I are 'as one', as one of my mothers-in-law would have said. Ruth, I truly love her. Sixteen years of pining for you, and five marriages in between, haven't hardened my heart, or indeed softened anything else. I'm just as fickle as ever – though not, I honestly believe, with Janice. She is IT. She also knows a quite remarkable amount about love for a lady who's been married a mere once. I intend to find out how. *You* probably know. I shall get you drunk so you tell me.

Next week I lose her to Wimbledon. How on earth did Janice manage to get hold of a debenture seat on the

Centre Court – for life? She refuses to say; merely shrugs. I don't recall Harry caring a toss about tennis.

In view of our 'union' it seemed apt to take her to *Les Liaisons Dangereuses* at the RSC. We got the last tickets for the last night. A friend of mine plays the seducer, the Vicomte de Valmont. He got the part because that is what he is in real life, so he has no need to act, which he can't anyway. But he is disgracefully handsome. I took Janice round to his dressing-room after the show, and that was nearly that. She was quite shameless: afterwards we had our first serious row. Fortunately a row can be a marvellous aphrodisiac, which I suspect is why several of my marriages lasted as long as they did.

Watching the play a thought came to me. The company is touring the production, starting in Madrid, as you doubtless know. I imagine you'll find yourself hostessing a reception for them in your First Lady capacity, with Piers droning on in welcome. My friend the 'Vicomte' would require only the slenderest of invitations to pursue you with lecherous ardour should you need the Chargé d'Affaires to have his nose rubbed in it further. With respect to your tedious husband, he is not in the same league as a seducer.

I may even be present to witness the spectacle, supposedly to write a piece on how an English play adapted from a French novel is received in Spain. God knows why my editor thinks his moronic readers give a fuck about any of this; none the less it may be Madrid for your veteran correspondent, alas without Janice who'll either be rooting for Andre Agassi or slicing salami in her deli.

I'll phone to say when I'm arriving, and where. It will be great to see you. Same restaurant?

Lots of love,

Tom.

Hacienda Monfrague
Plasencia

June 26th

Dear Janice,

This may be the first time I've written a letter topless. Estelle claims she does it all the time, but anatomical distribution makes it easier in her case: boobs impair the free movement of the arm as well as the line of vision. Whatever else Nautilus achieved, I am left with a decided thrust. Esteban responds likewise, further impeding my efforts to write to you. Pleasures can sometimes make life difficult, but my God it's wonderful to have some.

Perhaps I should begin at the beginning – the safe arrival of your diplomatic package, much appreciated as well as put to excellent use. Esteban particularly enjoys the Glow in the Dark variety, though it does make him look as if he's strolled off the set of *Star Wars.* Unfortunately, being Spanish he didn't understand what I meant by 'may the force be with you', though I must say he acted the part well enough.

There's something about a man advancing upon you with a luminous prick which is erotic and comic at the same time. Why not suggest it to Tom?

I keep digressing. The package of course arrived at the embassy, and was duly placed in the Chargé d'Affaires' 'In' tray – appropriate, I suppose, considering the contents. Piers noticed it was addressed to me, and with admirable good manners brought it home in his briefcase. Due to the golden crown on the wrapper he assumed, he said, that it must be some token of appreciation arranged through one of Estelle's royal connections. 'Absolutely,' I agreed, 'and very nice it is to be appreciated in this way.' I wished I hadn't said that because Piers grew curious about what was in the package, and I was forced to change the subject rapidly to the forthcoming visit of the Royal Shakespeare Company.

Relations with Piers have been more than usually brittle since his weekend with tweetie-pie. My sarcasm and Piers' guilt make an unhappy mix. Furthermore, on this particular day Tom's letter had arrived together with his article about my social and other triumphs in Madrid. The awful thing is, Piers still hasn't seen it. The paper was all over the news-stands; everyone kept ringing me up; people even recognised me in the street; and the one person in all Spain to remain totally unaware was my husband who was supposed to be driven wild with admiration and jealousy. Subsequently I learnt that only 'quality' papers are delivered to the embassy (I must get that changed forthwith); and since Piers walks round Madrid with his head in the clouds I decided I needed actually to thrust the paper under his nose. So I did. And would you believe it?: there it was, a double-page spread devoted to Ruth Conway's startling triumph and beauty, with accompanying glamorous photo of me apparently chatting up our future Queen. And what does Piers say? 'Not a particularly good photo of Di, is it? She's much prettier than that. Whoever sent you this anyway?' 'Tom Brand,' I replied fiercely. 'He wrote it. Look!' 'Oh, him! Really!' Piers said. 'I didn't think royalty was his line.' And he turned the page.

He hadn't even noticed the article was about me at all.

I was too flabbergasted to utter a word. My husband has to be the least aware man in the entire western hemisphere. I'm sure he still thinks Madonna is the Virgin Mary. I know he believes AIDS is about famine relief. And can I ever forget the day however long ago it was when he said 'Tell me, darling, that singer they're all talking about who just died: who was he?' The singer was Elvis Presley.

My only hope was to leave the paper prominently exposed next to his embassy papers before I left for my weekend tryst. Or maybe there's someone in the British Embassy who actually allows his eyes to drop below the level of *The Times* crossword.

Piers departed for work the next morning wishing me a pleasant few days. I think he still believes it's all to do with fund-raising. It gave me a happy feeling of revenge to be taking the same car he'd used for his weekend with tweetie-pie. I fancied I could still smell her, and promptly laid her ghost with a squirt of Giorgio. Then I drove off into the afternoon heat. No sex for three months did more for my appetite than for my driving. I thought about Esteban naked: dark, handsome and hairy. 'It doesn't matter if he's thick, my dear,' said Estelle on the phone, 'so long as he's thick in the right place.' The truck-driver who swerved forgave me when he saw the smile on my face. I blew him a kiss and he swerved again. A French driver behind me burnt the road with his brakes. Then Extremadura opened up before me and everything looked virile, like an ad for Marlboro Country – black bulls, bare mountains, rocks standing in water, muscled olive-trees. Everything was a penis or a cunt. The Home Counties isn't like this, I said to myself, or perhaps I just haven't noticed. I played a tape of flamenco dances, and snapped my fingers over the steering-wheel. Ruth was out a-hunting.

It takes a woman of mature years, I decided, to feel as unashamedly sexy as this. Tweetie-pie must be full of youthful inhibitions: I had none. None at all.

The hacienda is white and ranch-like, sprawled across a ridge overlooking a river valley with a line of rough hills beyond. A plume of dust blurred the rear-mirror as I left the Plasencia road. I saw Esteban's BMW parked by the entrance, and he must have heard me coming because he appeared round the side of the house. He was togged up in riding-gear – immaculate, perfectly scrubbed, like a male model in a Jaeger catalogue. I could tell he'd spent half the day preparing for this entrance: he certainly hadn't been anywhere near a horse in case he got a hair on his shirt.

It was a strange moment. There we were face to face – me in shirt and tatty jeans, he dressed for the Badminton Horse Trials. There was only one thing on my mind: I was here to be fucked, preferably very soon, and thereafter a great deal. Presumably he had the same thought: he'd been insinuating as much for several months. OK, so we're now facing one another in front of his love-nest amid the majestic solitude of Extremadura. The world is holding its breath.

And what do we do? We shake hands.

Relationships follow predestinate grooves, don't they? And Spain is a formal country. The handshake was only the beginning. A well-buttoned matron appeared – she had been Esteban's nurse, I learnt – and silently took my suitcase. A younger woman of similar proportions (her daughter?) lowered her head in greeting as we entered the house. I followed the large bum of Nanny Esteban along a corridor. The master followed quietly behind. A door was opened. This was the first shock. We were in separate bedrooms.

It was seven in the evening. I was left alone. I had a private bathroom, and the view from my window was spectacular – wild country with a thread of a river winding through it before disappearing between low hills that were deep gold in the sun. A pair of Palamino horses were shaking their manes in a paddock not far from the house. These would be for tomorrow: Estelle had warned me. I felt grateful at last to my mother for all those point-to-points she insisted I enter as a teenager, my bulges imprisoned behind autumnal tweeds and pony-club tie, my hair crammed into a net beneath a hat that would have withstood the walls of Jericho.

'Drinks at eight,' Esteban had said, leaving me here. I tried to figure it out. Seduction weekend? Could such a thing really be written into the rules of this house? Or were we to wait until nanny, nanny's daughter, butler, cook and God knows who else had retired to the servants' quarters, then tiptoe into lust along silent corridors?

There was a knock on the door as I was undressing, and Nanny Jnr. rustled into the room and turned down the bed, heaving a grey bum in my direction. She rustled out again and the door clicked quietly. It was seven-fifteen. I ran a bath, then laid out the dress I'd brought – a dreamy, floaty number in ice-blue chiffon, a 'not-quite-of-this-world' look which I imagined an earthy Spaniard would appreciate, and very shortly remove. But now I wasn't quite so sure: I felt I should at least have borrowed a tiara from Estelle. I looked at the package containing the condoms and wondered if I might cut out the crown on the wrapper instead.

As the evening progressed I began to think a lot about Estelle. This, I now understood, was the tight-lipped Spain she had broken away from. Esteban and she obeyed the same social formalities – drinks on a silver tray at sundown, waiter in stiff black and white breathing rhythmically through his nose, a little hand-bell to summon service. But Estelle would have been naked. Esteban was trapped within his charcoal suit.

Dinner was the two of us together under a shroud of silence. Plates were whisked away and replaced, accompanied by more breathing through the nose. Esteban commented from time to time on the regional specialities, on the wine, the estate, his childhood here, his parents' childhood here: I began to sense that this empty room seated his entire family since the expulsion of Napoleon. I had dabbed my pulse-spots with Jean Patou's 'Joy': now I could feel 'Joy' being smothered by a pall of ancestral dust. The servants came, and coughed, and went. A clock ticked to ten. Eleven. Eleven-thirty.

We reached the final course. I looked across the long table at Esteban. It was like gazing at a prisoner through the grille: the jailers were hovering, listening, vanishing discreetly just beyond the door, and listening.

I suppose I should have waited. There may be a time for everything, but I've never been good at that. Sometimes only *now* will do, and this was such a time.

What did it matter if I shocked Esteban's nanny, or his nanny's nanny, or his ancestral ghosts? Let it be. I offered a silent greeting to Estelle and pushed the beautifully-wrapped package of condoms across the table. And while Esteban was undoing it in some surprise, I caused him further surprise by removing all my clothes. I have no idea if the jailers were witnesses to the next few minutes or not, nor did I much care; but I need to tell you that my first fuck for three months was celebrated against a soft cushion of Tarta de Santa Teresa, a local speciality made of apricots which I'm sure would have been only a little less pleasurable than the fuck had my priorities been otherwise. But then St Teresa was always good at self-sacrifice, and I feel sure she would have approved.

Things changed from then on. We had a vigorous night with the help of your enterprising shopping in Soho, and I woke late saying to myself – 'Well, I've got a beautiful young lover.'

Esteban had become wonderfully released from his chains. Nanny and daughter, if they knew of the palace revolution, continued to behave as if nothing could ever change. (I did wonder what they thought about the condition of the Tarta de Santa Teresa when they came to clear the table.) They both of them waved the young master and his elegant lady off riding rather late in the morning, and Extremadura passed gently beneath our Palaminos' hooves. There were bright poppies in the fields, and azure-winged magpies darted noisily between the cork-oaks. It was hot. We spoke little, but every so often Esteban would glance tenderly at me as we rode. It was a time of ease.

Before long we reached the river I'd spotted from my window. It ran between rocks and sandbanks, deep and inviting pools forming between them. We tied our horses to a tree that overhung the water, and bathed naked. Esteban has the body of an athlete – heavy-chested, slim-hipped, powerful legs. We dived from the rocks, embraced in the water, laughed. I felt free as air. Esteban had brought a picnic, and we dried off in the sun munching *chorizos*, bread and goat's cheese, and drinking home-made wine. Then we lay in the sun, sated with the night and the day, weary with wine and heat. I thought of Piers and tweetie-pie sneaking intimacies among bound volumes of *The Illustrated London News*, smiled and fell asleep.

Siestas in the sun aren't like ordinary sleep. You don't dream; you go out dead to the world – anaesthetised – and wake surprised. My head was on Esteban's thigh, and when I opened my eyes all I could see were his balls. I gazed at them for a while, then reached out and felt the weight of them: they reminded me of mangoes' stones, elongated and flattish. How curious it must be, I thought, to have all that dangling between one's legs; how does a man walk? I wondered if I ought to put Ambre Solaire on them: sunburnt balls must be terribly painful. But I couldn't reach without running the risk of waking him, and he was sleeping so beautifully.

Then I glanced up at the sky, and suddenly I remembered Estelle's words, 'You will see many vultures.' My God, she was right. There were twenty of them at least circling round and round immediately above us. Perhaps they imagined we were dead. I didn't at all fancy being torn apart, so I took hold of the nearest thing which happened to be Esteban's prick and began to wave it about, hoping the vultures would get the message; they've got astonishing eyesight, Piers once told me. Well, I don't know if the vultures reacted, but the prick certainly did. It stiffened hugely – an enormous thing. I'd only seen it illuminated at night before. This was too much. I came down on him; leaned over him, brushing his chest-hairs with my breasts. That seemed to wake him. At any rate he clasped my bosom quite violently, and exploded inside me. It was incredible. All my former loves passed before my eyes. I saw stars, comets, meteors, the lot – I even heard bells ringing. And how those bells did ring. On and on. It was a while before I realised why. We were surrounded by sheep, hundreds and hundreds of them. They made rustling, pattering sounds as they moved around us, munching.

It was all rather magical in an odd sort of way, until my pastoral idyll was interrupted by a thought. Sheep means shepherd. And at that moment I heard him whistling. Esteban heard him too. This was no moment for post-coital afterplay. We dressed in haste. Esteban got his pubic hairs caught in his zip, and I laughed. He didn't. The shepherd said '*Buenas tardes*' and wandered by whistling.

And now I'm sitting here in the garden, sunburnt and sore. Esteban has gone off to do something manly with the horses: I can hear his voice. Tonight, I guess, we may just sleep, unless of course Esteban insists. I hope so.

Then tomorrow it's home, if you can call it that. And battle resumes. I wonder which of us had the better weekend away, Piers or me. I'm certain of one thing: he's never had his prick waved at a vulture. Nor will he have screwed tweetie-pie on a Tarta de Santa Teresa: at least I sincerely hope not.

But will he finally have seen Tom's article about me? I imagine I'll soon know.

Do tell Tom, if he's not already on his way, that I'd love to see him. And you know, Janice, I'm so happy for you. All that smiling you can't stop: I know how it feels. You deserve some happiness. I've at least stolen some.

With much love
Ruth.

1 River Mews

June 30th

Dearest Ruth,

Your wonderful and disgraceful letter arrived this morning. Do you think that with a subtle change of ingredients I could include Tarta de Santa Teresa in

Prawnography? The illustration could get the book banned worldwide, of course, and even Samuel Johnson might understand what was being laid on top of the shortcrust pastry.

It's true, by the way, what Tom said. We do have a mega-contract from the States. The publisher isn't entirely happy about my illustration for Stuffed Mussels – not on moral grounds as I'd imagined, but fear of libel. Apparently the muscled lady being stuffed in my picture looks too much like a notoriously litigious movie-star who happens also to be lesbian; so I have to rework it. I did say rather timidly when he phoned late the other evening, 'What about the bible belt?' and his response was, 'Fuck the bible belt: they only buy bibles anyway.' So I suggested a *Ribald Bible* as a follow-up. He laughed and said he'd think about it. Ten minutes later he rang back: 'What about *The Acts of the Apostles* – Unexpurgated?'

Tom has just left for Spain – and you. And I have to say to you, Ms Conway, 'Don't you dare!' I know he's lusted after you for sixteen years, but it's now too late. He belong 'a me.

I want to be serious. I'm just a teeny-weeny bit enormously in love. He's everything I imagined I'd never want. I used to wake up in the morning with a picture in my head of the perfect man for me. He was always slim and dark, a bit younger than I am, quiet and serious, perhaps a scholar or a poet, single of course, never married because the right woman never came along, just enough turbulent affairs with the wrong women so he'd recognise me instantly. Oh, and rather sober, a non-smoker of course, very good around the house, very good with all my friends without ever making a pass at them, and shyly looking forward to being a father.

And what do I get? A grey-haired, hard-smoking old drunk who's been married five times and has screwed just about every woman I know, has three children already and claims no longer to have 'enough of the little wrigglies' to father any more. Great, isn't it!

But then in the mornings, if Tom's away, I slot in my mental picture of Mr Perfect and I say to myself – 'Jesus, how dull.'

Tom is *never* dull – not even when he's talking about his wives. Oh Ruth, am I really going to be another one? It might be a better recipe for permanence if I wasn't.

But please send him back safe.

My love to you, and of a different sort (which you're *not* to give) to Tom,

Janice.

PS Wimbledon all next week. Ching has given me the whole week off. I wish he'd stop telling all his customers I'm doing this wonderful cookery book. Do you think I ought to use a pseudonym?

PPS Clive loves the local comprehensive. He's become a model child. I wonder if he'll turn out to be very ordinary. It might be a relief.

MADRID 1800 HRS JUNE 30
CABLE DESPATCH TO: JANICE BLAKEMORE
ONE RIVER MEWS LONDON W4 UK HEREWITH
MARITAL REPAIRS SERVICE REPORT NUMBER
FIVE STOP IMBECILIC HUSBAND WRAPPED
NEWSPAPER AROUND ERRANT DOGSHIT
UNREAD STOP BACK SQUARE ONE STOP TOM
JUST ARRIVED UNRECOGNISABLE IN LOVE
ENVIOUS CONGRATULATIONS
SOD PIERS STOP RUTH

July

British Embassy
Madrid

July 1st

Dear Harry,

You puzzle me. When your marriage with Janice was at its most explosive you wrote cheerful and amusing letters. Now you are a free man, wallowing in double-baths with senators' wives or laying the entire female press corps, you write miserably. You are of a most perverse disposition.

As for waxing indignant over Janice choosing an older man, this becomes you even less. Women often choose older men, and one day you will doubtless be grateful that they do. Without wishing to sound pompous – though I know I am – age can bring a certain maturity of outlook to a relationship, which women frequently value more highly than they do sex. Angelica and I have grown close enough since our buoyant weekend in Toledo to be able to discuss this subject freely. She is fully aware of my unswerving commitment to Ruth, and under these circumstances I am more than ever convinced that a sexual liaison would both distress and confuse Angelica, tempted though I sometimes am to take advantage of her trusting nature.

For instance, we had dinner at her place the other evening, her relatives being away, and after she had taken a shower she wandered into the living-room wrapped in only the flimsiest of towels. I had to exert considerable self-control, especially when I became aware that she possesses the most delectable breasts. At her suggestion we may take a further weekend away, this time in Malaga: I know how fond she is of bathing. Frankly, I find it hard to refuse her anything she wants, and she was delightfully insistent. Of course she has little money of her own, and on British Council pay would certainly be unable to afford the trip south on her own. She awarded me an exuberant kiss by way of thanks, somehow retaining a hold on most of her towel as she did so. She really is a pure joy. I must take the greatest care not to let things get out of hand, and it worries me that Ruth remains convinced it has already done so. She simply will not listen.

Ruth's own social life appears constantly on the boil. She works intensely hard at her fund-raising, and came back quite exhausted last weekend, none the less managing a most appealing sun-tan. Apparently much of her business was conducted out of doors, and she spoke enthusiastically of the local scenery and wild-life. She also told a delightful story about vultures, and having to wave the nearest upright thing in order to convince the creatures she was not a corpse. Knowing Ruth, the nearest upright thing was probably a wine bottle. At any rate she assured me that whatever it was did the trick to perfection.

The staff here keep telling me of an article about her which appeared in the popular press recently. Unfortunately I never got a chance to see it, and Ruth modestly never kept a copy. The only tabloid rag I have set eyes on for a while had a piece by your friend Tom Brand about Princess Di, which found an appropriate use disposing of a mess deposited by our neighbour's revolting Pekinese.

Conway's Law is once again under strain, this time due to a visit by the Royal Shakespeare Company. I was required to attend the first night with all medals flying, and this evening the usual 'cultural brotherhood' speech will get another airing at an embassy reception.

A new ambassador has been appointed, and may shortly disturb me with a reconnaissance visit. He is said to be fluent in Urdu – so much more useful here than my Spanish: the Foreign Office can always be relied upon to recognise what qualifications are really vital. I am now threatened with Haiti, where the only common language is the hand-grenade; but after sixteen years living with Ruth such things hold few terrors.

Your humour seems to have deteriorated into bad puns. My weekend in Toledo was *not* entirely devoted to addressing the question 'To lay or not to lay', though I have to admit there were moments by the pool when it did arise – the question, I mean.

With best wishes.

Yours,

Piers.

93 Avenida de Cervantes
Madrid

July 1st (and in about
ten minutes it will be July 2nd)

Dear Janice,

I can't sleep, it's much too hot and I'm much too sober. So I shall take you calmly through the events of the past three days. Selected events, that is; I shan't spend time on the phone calls from Esteban which would certainly qualify as sexual harassment under the new E.C. laws had I not already harassed him so successfully on the ancestral dining-table.

The RSC duly arrived earlier in the week, to be greeted formally at Madrid airport by Piers, and less formally by me – but at least I was upright this time. There was no difficulty spotting Tom's friend who plays the Vicomte de Valmont: beauty rarely graces a male countenance quite so shamelessly. To judge by their expressions at least five wives in the reception party swore to commit serious adultery before the man even set foot on the tarmac. What fascinates me is how it's invariably the ones you'd least expect who wet their knickers. I was unusually reticent; but when Tom re-introduced me in the VIP lounge (how the hell did he get there?) I became unashamedly the sixth candidate, determined to pull rank if necessary in order to jump the queue. You saw *Les Liaisons Dangereuses* in London, so you'll understand, and from Tom's account you almost had an Undressing Room scene after the show.

Wednesday was the First Night: Piers stiff as a waxwork, all Madrid present in its finery, divided as far as I could judge between those who imagined they were watching Shakespeare, and those who couldn't understand enough English to know what they were watching anyway. Piers was wearing his Head of Mission expression which he's been rehearsing for years: I know it well. It usually means he'd give anything to be roaming the hills in knee-length shorts looking for rare orchids – only these days I doubt if it's orchids he dreams of plucking. I was dressed to justify the reputation Tom awarded me in his article: Caroline Charles emerald-green skirt, long and straight, with tiny strappy top and jangly earrings. All perfectly demure from the front for greeting ministers and the like, but with an outrageous slit at the back as a parting quip (or quim). Being satin, everything rustled as I moved, like a hundred whispers. I was pleased to notice there were plenty of those too, and particularly pleased that Piers noticed.

'I suppose they've all seen that article about you,' he said huffily.

'Maybe they've just seen *me*,' I retorted.

'They can certainly see a lot of you,' he added, having just observed the slit; 'usually it's the front.'

'I'll reserve that for Saturday,' I said, thinking of the embassy reception where I had every intention of vamping the most gorgeous actor in England, preferably in front of my less-than-gorgeous husband. 'At least it'll distract people from your speech – not that it would be difficult.'

'Whatever's the perfume you're wearing?' he asked, ignoring the jibe.

I smiled: 'Poison. Christian Dior. It almost annihilates your aftershave.'

I was beginning to recognise one of those bitchy marital dialogues we always vowed we'd never have. I even felt like announcing to the various nobs I was being introduced to – 'Yes, I *am* the Chargé d'Affaires' wife: his mistress couldn't come – which is not usually her problem, so I'm told.'

That evening I was the closest I've ever been to hating Piers. For the first time I could sense the erosion of so much I've always taken for granted between us. The sap was draining out of our life; it was beginning to taste bitter, and I could imagine how in a few years that bitterness would become etched in my face. I'd become one of those acid queens who feed on blame and haven't had a good fuck or a good laugh in years. Women with arthritis of the heart – tight-lipped, tight between the legs, but never of course tight.

This mustn't happen, I thought. It mustn't, and it won't. I'd leave Piers rather than that. Perhaps even within a couple of weeks I might leave him, when my One Hundred Days is up. Leave him with his child-lover. Why not? He'd soon learn to change nappies.

The curtain went up for the second act. You remember, it's the bit when we begin to realise just how deadly Madame de Merteuil is at manipulating everyone around her, including the Vicomte de Valmont. God, I thought, that's *real* power, to be able to twist round one's little finger a man as gorgeously dangerous as Valmont. And there was Piers sitting next to me, po-faced, a novice by comparison, a mere tenderfoot; now if I'd been Mme de

Merteuil he'd be dancing to any tune I cared to play, and she certainly wouldn't need any exercise machines, star signs or flattering newspaper articles to do her work for her. She'd just do it. Wham!

It was then it came to me. I shall be Mme de Merteuil. Why not? I've got the looks, I've got the low cunning, and by God I've got the motivation. All I needed was a game-plan. I watched her coolly manoeuvring Valmont, steering him around like a croupier steers betting chips, then dangling irresistible temptations before his libido. And the next moment there he was seducing the innocent young Cécile on stage before my eyes. Ruthless, deadly he was; she all fluttering heart and fluttering petticoats. Not a hope.

But of course; that was it! I laughed aloud. Piers gave me a sideways look. Saturday's reception at the embassy – the perfect setting. Mme de Merteuil would do her good work, and Valmont would do her bidding. The woman to be seduced didn't have to be me – at least not yet. It could be someone else: someone more youthful, more impressionable, just like Cécile. If a flower is to be picked, then let it be a budding rose, best of all somebody else's budding rose. Ideal.

I continued to laugh and smile all the way through the rest of the play, and clapped vigorously at the end. 'Did you really think it was as good as that?' enquired Piers as we jostled out of the theatre. 'Most certainly,' I said. 'I feel quite refreshed. I see the world with new eyes.' Piers gave me a strange look.

And there in the foyer, thank God, was Tom. 'Ring me tomorrow morning – urgently,' I whispered.

Piers and I returned to our separate rooms. I remembered it was almost July, and there'd be a new tweetie-pie on the calendar. I had a look out of curiosity. Oh yes, she was exactly the part. Slim. Blonde. High-breasted. Pert nipples raised (Estelle would have approved); head tilted back in the sun, hair dragging in the sand, legs parted. She was being fucked by the camera. Well, I thought, I can persuade Valmont to do better than that, and he can bring his own long lens with him. Oh tweetie-pie, if luck is on my side Friday is going to be the night of your life.

Tom duly rang the next morning, and we arranged to meet in a café off the Gran Via. I slipped two invitations for the embassy reception into my pocket. Tom was waiting with a what's-she-up-to-now look on his face, and ordered brandy with his coffee. It was blistering hot in the street, and clusters of tourists were trying to cool themselves with little flamenco fans they'd bought in the hotel gift-shop. Tom sipped his brandy and waited.

'Will you do me a favour – today?' I said. Tom gave me one of his lopsided smiles. 'I've waited sixteen years to do you a favour, and now I'm unavailable, you ask me. What?'

I produced the two invitations. One of them invited 'Mr Tom Brand'; the other was blank. I didn't even know the little tart's name – except Angelica. 'Angelica Tweetie-Pie' (an old Scottish family?) mightn't get her past the embassy door. I began to explain carefully. I wanted him to go to the British Council library, waste whatever time he needed among the English newspapers, ask whatever inane questions a visiting journalist might be expected to ask, and then pounce. 'Not literally, Tom;

you're far too ancient and would frighten the kitten away. No, tell her your actor-friend gave you this spare invitation – she's sure to know about him – and would she perhaps like it?'

'And what if she says "No", she's got a date?'

'She won't. The only man she dates as far as I know is my bloody husband, and he's going to be there anyway boring everyone to death.'

'And then?'

'You do your match-making bit with your friend. You know how to sweet-talk young women, Tom. Better still, you actually bring her to the party so she doesn't get snaffled up by some panting Italian first. OK?'

And I gave him my *Liaisons Dangereuses* smile. Tom just looked at me.

'And when I've finished pimping for you, what's in it for me, may I ask?'

I laid a fond hand on his wrist (don't get me wrong, it was Mme de Merteuil's hand, not mine).

'I'll put in a good word for you to Janice,' I said. 'I won't tell her how you once screwed the winner of the Eurovision Song Contest.' (And now I *have* told you, but I bet he has already – he's terribly proud of it.)

Tom gave me another one-sided smile.

'You beautiful bitch.'

And he got up, leaving me the bill.

Change of scene. Thirty-six hours later. This evening. Dusk. The garden of the British Embassy is choked with *notorati.* Piers is doing his worst to be charming. The cast is getting exuberantly drunk. Xavier is there looking patrician. Foreign diplomats are looking at their watches, and Esteban is looking at my breasts – I'm wearing my low-cut Bruce Oldfield number; Mme de Merteuil would have been proud of me. I play my part well, keeping a sharp eye on Valmont, hoping he won't get too pissed, or swept up by one of the vampires who are flapping around him. One Egyptian houri is performing a sort of snake-dance as she talks, and I have to do my First Lady act, dragging her off to meet a member of the Polish trade delegation: that should cool her off. I just wish Tom would hurry up. I'm also longing (dreading) to set eyes on tweetie-pie.

Then – there he is; and that must be her with him. God, she's pretty. Got the nerve to wear T-shirt and jeans – got the nerve because she's got the body. I *hate* the young. For a moment I feel like going up to her and saying, 'OK, you win.'

Then I remember – Ruth, you're Mme de Merteuil; what would she do? She would watch. So I watch. I exchange glances with Tom. I see him steering the girl towards Valmont. Tom is introducing her: it's like watching a goldfish being introduced to a pike. Go on! Go on! Devour her! And now Piers is on the terrace waiting to speak: I wonder if he's spotted tweetie-pie. He won't have any idea she's here.

No one listens to the speech: they've all heard it many times before. Valmont wouldn't be listening even if he hadn't heard it before: his eyes are gobbling up tweetie-pie. I want to jump up and down with joy, but my breasts will jump out if I do, so I restrain myself. It's dark by now. The lights in the embassy garden make the scene look like a Renoir. I move a little closer to see better. Tom has vanished. Piers is still droning on. Valmont is turning away: Oh no! Then I catch sight of his hand brushing her breast as he leaves. Relief. She seems to be leaving too, by another route – how discreet of them. Valmont is heading my way. My dress halts his practised eyes just long enough. I tell him what a superb performance he gave the other night (I almost add I hope he'll give an even better performance tonight). I remind him we already met at the airport, and tell him who I am. I can see his mental computer at work: does all this make me available or unavailable? His eyes look hungry, but I'm determined not to make him fancy me more than tweetie-pie. So I move out of reach: he's obviously a tit-man.

I then invite him for coffee in the flat in the morning, and scrawl the address on his invitation card. It couldn't seem more like an assignation, could it? Never mind: so he's lining me up next. At least he's sure to turn up. His eyes undress me and he leaves a little reluctantly: one bird is already in the hand – the bush can wait.

Esteban meanwhile is looking stormy and proprietorial. Piers is winding up, thanking all the people he's never heard of.

End of scene.

Now, Janice, I shall go out and have a one AM brandy in the Plaza Mayor, posting this letter on the way. I love these Spanish midsummer nights – so long as I'm not trying to sleep. I trust Valmont isn't either.

I shall sit patiently like Mme de Merteuil – or perhaps it should be Mme Defarge, knitting my rival's downfall and remembering that one of Piers' fellow-Arians was Joseph Ignace Guillotin.

It's time for blood,
and for much love,
Ruth.

PS If Valmont is early tomorrow he'll be hoping to seduce me. If he's late he's already seduced the girl. Of course both may be true in either case. I shall let you know.

1 River Mews

July 4th

Dearest Ruth,

I phoned this morning the moment I got your letter. But no answer. And no answer at midday either. I couldn't even get hold of Tom at the hotel. Whatever is going on?

All this agony over a piece of flotsam. You know, when I last spoke to Tom he said you've only got to look at the girl to see she's a star-fucker. Piers is nuts. Well, he's got two weeks before Waterloo to come to his senses. Meanwhile, good luck with *Les Liaisons Dangereuses.*

So, I find myself alone again. No sooner do I meet a man I want to share my life with than he gets detained as a spy on someone else's mistress. Are you sure, my wicked friend, you're not hijacking Tom just in case? Please send him home soon. I miss him.

So does Clive. He admires Tom hugely – not for being handsome and wise and generous and funny, but for having been married five times. 'How long will *you* last, Mummy?' he said yesterday, the beast; then a bit later – 'Tom must know an awful lot about girls, Mummy; do you think he'd teach me if I asked him?' He told Tom very solemnly he now has nine pubic hairs. Tom said he'd better wait a bit.

There have been mixed reactions in River Mews to Tom moving in. Ah-man-dah gushed, then said he looked just like her father – the bitch. The Creepy Crawleys tried to come to tea. Nina wanted to know if he played tennis. Louisa was quite certain she'd met him once at a Rosicrucian gathering in Acton.

Lottie's reaction was the saddest. 'Oh dear,' she said, 'how lucky you are.' Attila, who moved in on her in a big way, is now swiftly moving out, taking his super-gun with him, husband Maurice having returned from Macclesfield with a lesser weapon. Well, the street will be a quieter place, and the mists of unhappiness will settle over Lottie once more.

Do you want to hear about Kevin? As you know, he can't stand Tom; but right now he has more serious preoccupations. Yin-and-Yang is pregnant: at least, one of them is. 'Better than both of them, Kevin,' I suggested. 'You aren't 'arf right there, darlin',' he said. 'At least I now know which is which.'

One person who's really delighted for me is Ching at the deli. 'A good man, Mr Tom,' he says very often. 'Time he got married.' I nod incredulously. Yesterday he pressed a Chinese recipe on me: 'for your sea-food cookery book; my wife she make beautifully.' I look at it, and he's dead right. Spicy Prawn Balls. I must tell Tom. 'You will show me please your drawing.' I'm not so sure about that. But at least Samuel Johnson will like it.

And now I shall stop prattling.

I think of you a lot. Tom's article was terrific, and you *are* everything he said. Hang on to that. Perhaps I could find a place for '*Tweetie Pie*' in *Prawnography*: 'Whip soundly and add to tart until completely smothered.' You know, Piers is going to feel an awful fool. Will you be able to cope? Can I help? Fly out?

You can help by telling Tom I love him. I think he knows, but tell him anyway. And tell his editor to fuck off.

It's sad being at Wimbledon without you. Last year we were celebrating my rotten marriage going right. This year my thoughts were of your good marriage going wrong.

With lots of love,
Janice.

Palacio Pizarro
Trujillo

July 4th

Dear Janice,

Marital Repairs Service Report No 6

I'm in hiding. My guardian angel is Estelle.

The key-hole window of my bedroom offers a fugitive's view of all Extremadura. How calm it looks. Hard to believe that not a million miles beyond those hills a tempest is raging. It's called Hurricane Piers, and he's in a mood to commit murder, starting with me. Meanwhile only Tom knows I'm here, and Estelle promises to deny all knowledge of my whereabouts. The portcullis is down, the drawbridge is up, and so is my blood-pressure. Only nine of my One Hundred Days remain, and on a current review of troops it doesn't look as if I'll even make it as far as Waterloo, let alone win a battle.

So, this is what happened after I posted my last letter to you. I had several brandies on that midsummer night: bad for the digestion but wondrous for the soul. The square was full of lovers with nowhere to go. I had a place to go but the man I love would be snoring by now. And the woman *he* loved would (I hoped) be having her petals strewn across a darkened room. Joseph Ignace Guillotin, do your good work.

I hardly slept that night. Piers did indeed snore: Spanish walls have big ears. Then it was Saturday morning, and sure enough there were the knickers hoisted opposite: a pink pair – it must have been a saint's day.

I knew Piers was due at some meeting around ten. Valmont was due here at eleven – a decent enough hour, I thought, for a man with a healthy appetite for the night.

Piers was in a foul temper. He did his yoga in the bathroom, and fell over. I heard him swear. This is nothing, I thought, to what he's going to say later. And suddenly I felt sorry for him. Was I being a bitch and a ball-breaker? Then I cast my mind back over the previous months – the pain, the jealousy, humiliation, helplessness, the sense of void, the collapse of everything I loved most deeply. How dare he have done all that to me? I'll pick up the pieces, but first let them fall.

He was still in a foul temper when he left for the embassy.

'Terrible manners, these bloody actors. In the middle of thanking them, and one of them slips away. I saw him last night.'

I don't believe he can have seen tweetie-pie at all. Then he departed, grumbling about the heat. I told him his next posting would probably be Iceland, but he just closed the door.

Valmont was only half an hour late, which I thought was a good sign. I cast a quick eye over him: beautiful actors can look very un-beautiful in the morning. Estelle claims she never draws back the curtains till midday for that reason. But Valmont had clearly found plenty of time to compose a dishevelled look – designer stubble, white espadrilles, shirt tucked in hastily enough for the folds to direct the eye downwards to the hugging jeans. At any other time, I thought; but this was not the time. Mme de Merteuil was on duty.

So I greeted him with a hand to kiss, not a cheek. Then I made coffee, produced some *tapas* and offered him a brandy which he refused with an actor's gesture. We were already playing our roles well.

I opened the exchange with a studied little speech in the eighteenth century manner. I was anxious, I said, to enquire about the innocent young lady in whom my husband had taken a certain protective interest. I had noticed the previous evening that *monsieur* escorted the lady from the embassy gathering, and wished to receive assurance that his intentions had been entirely honourable, and her innocence respected.

The surprised look on Valmont's face quickly vanished, and he was gazing at me intently.

'After all, sir,' I added quietly, 'I understand you have a certain reputation with ladies, though in this instance I'm quite sure your sense of propriety would have been uppermost' (God, I hoped that was *not* what was uppermost).

His face had taken on a studied look, and I noticed he was now standing precisely as he did on the stage: hands clasped, one foot before the other, head turned to offer me a Byronic half-profile.

'I'm delighted, madam, to assure you' – he softened his voice like velvet – 'that the young lady parted with nothing that had not already been willingly proferred to others. In fact I found her to be endowed with surprising talents for one so young: her education has certainly not been neglected, and I pride myself that I will have furthered that education, not detracted from it. I trust you find that to be a satisfactory answer.'

And he gave a little bow, one hand behind his back, an imaginary handkerchief in the other. He was doing wonderfully well not to smile. I managed to conceal my own delight, and decided to play the game a while longer.

'Thank you, sir,' I said. 'I'm relieved to know the nature of your encounter, and I look forward to informing my husband of the excellent care you have taken of his protégée.'

He bowed again, took a final sip of coffee, and picked up a non-existent hat as he prepared to leave.

'I understand, madam, that the young lady in question is quite as well known to your husband as she is to me. Indeed, our mutual friend Mr Brand informs me that she is currently his mistress.' He took a few measured steps towards the door, then paused with his hand on the handle. 'And I think you may rest assured that she performs that role exceedingly well. Your husband is in good hands. I wish you good day, dear madam.'

A final bow, and he left.

Well, I suppose I shouldn't have expected an amateur Mme de Merteuil to be able to outplay a professional Valmont. I should stick to real life.

But at least I knew. Oh thank you, thank you, Valmont. I was so overjoyed I wanted to ring up and tell everyone – you, Tom, Estelle. But what about Piers? How was I going to break the news to him; and how would he react?

I was expecting him home for lunch. I felt as though I'd suspended an axe over the door. He returned in an unusually jolly mood. He'd been speaking to the new ambassador on the phone. Bough, his name is: known in the trade as BOF, 'Boring Old Fart'. Piers was chuckling.

This made it more difficult. It was like the old Piers, the man I loved. The man I still loved. How could I do this to him? Again I made myself think of the misery of those months, what he'd done to me. It wasn't the infidelity – if it had been that I'd be the one under the axe. It was the loving, the fact that he *loved* her. That was the betrayal. Love isn't something you can share. I came close to it with Jean-Claude in Athens, but I saw the danger signals and drew back: Piers was my man, my bond, my life. I never even intended to tell him about Jean-Claude until I found out he'd screwed his own secretary. She wasn't even attractive, which made it worse. We were furious with one another and then made love all weekend. That's always been our life together, and somehow it's worked – better than most people's lives.

So I told him about Valmont. There was a huge and terrible silence. Then he exploded. I've never seen Piers like that. The worst was that I realised he really did love the girl, in an idealistic sort of way. She was like an icon to him, and I'd smashed it.

He didn't believe it, he said. It was a foul lie. How dare I? It was a plot I'd hatched with that dreadful man Tom Brand who'd always been sniffing around me like a bloodhound. He would never forgive me for this. Angelica was pure, innocent, he'd never even been to bed with her – had no intention to: he'd always tried to tell me this, but I'd never listen. I never listened to anything. He'd had enough. I'd stooped too low. This was the end.

I thought he was going to smash the place up. I thought he was going to hit me. Then I burst into tears. But he only swore at me, and stormed out. The last thing he said was – 'You've fucked every man in sight ever since I met you: that's all you ever think about. You don't know anything about love at all. Well, I do. Goodbye.'

Two hours and several drinks later I collected myself and a few belongings together. I phoned Estelle. She promised Xavier would send round a car straightaway. I was to come here.

I hardly remember the drive. My eyes needed windscreen wipers.

That was the day before yesterday. By today I felt calmer. My window looks out over miles of peace. And Estelle talked to me through the night. 'It's all right, my dear,' she said. 'It's Luis's night off. He should see his wife sometimes, don't you agree?' She held my hands, and I was grateful. 'Piers is just another fool,' she insisted. 'He'll find out the truth. Have patience. In the meanwhile I have had a word with Juan Carlos.'

I couldn't help laughing.

So there we are. What now? I don't know where I go from here. I'm licking my wounds, and shall phone Tom later in Madrid. You don't mind my leaning on him, do you? I need my friends right now.

I also need a drink. I'll raise a glass to you, dear friend.

With much love,
Ruth.

Some bar or other
Madrid

July 9th

My darling Janice,

I used to find Piers tediously sane: suddenly he's become endearingly insane. In fact he's totally lost his marbles. I received an apoplectic phone call first thing this morning accusing me of spreading slanderous tales about his little piece of crumpet. Not that he described her in exactly those terms – more like the Virgin Mary reborn. He could hardly get the words out, he was so furious. Ruth was every bit as bad as me, he raged; we were both muck-rakers, decadents, perverts, too jaded to recognise virtue and goodness when we saw it; we should be ashamed of ourselves, etc., etc.

This was altogether too much. So when he paused for breath I told him the truth, and if he didn't believe me to go and confront the girl himself.

There was a terrible silence; then he put down the receiver. I hope he hasn't shot himself: the death-toll among embassy staff here is already well over the yearly quota.

And now of course you want to know what the truth is, don't you? Where shall I pick up the story? I told you on the phone about Ruth's little exercise in procuring with the assistance of my RSC friend who is playing Valmont. (Remember him? Of course you bloody well do.)

Well, it worked. Being addicted to gossip, I went and had a drink with him in his dressing-room, and using all the discretion for which I'm well known made enquiries about Piers' sweet little thing. 'Very religious, so I understand.' A look of surprise overtook him. 'Can't say we talked about God much,' he said, 'though we managed to explore quite a few other mysteries. Not that they were exactly mysteries,' he went on. 'The girl may be only twenty but she knows as many tricks as a Saigon tart.'

(How they do travel, these actors. Culture is a truly wonderful thing.)

She makes no bones about her private life apparently. The girl had come out here to get away from hot-gospelling parents (hence the name Angelica), and to have a good time. She even keeps count: 'Valmont' was her thirteenth in the six months she's been here. I commiserated on thirteen being an unlucky number, but he looked a little miffed; he seemed to think his prowess had been devalued, and wishes he'd made a pitch for Ruth instead.

It remains something of a mystery what the girl saw

in Piers. I know you've often said how sexy he is. Perhaps it's just sexual power-broking on her part – seeing if she can get the Head of Mission into the missionary position. If so, she failed.

So there you are: there's the dirt. I'm left with a sense of wonderment at the need some men feel to idealise women, embalm them in purity. I trust I don't do that with you: purity is not something I know much about.

Anyway, I phoned Ruth – very sensibly in hiding while the storm blows – and reported all this. And do you know, she actually felt sorry for Piers. A woman's love can be infuriatingly splendid. How's yours?

I shall be home in just over a week, I promise. My editor is at last convinced there's no royal scandal to report, or even invent. But perhaps I'm just past it. If *Prawnography* makes it I may take early retirement and devote myself to preparing irresistible delicacies for the lady I love.

Do you really want more children? I was only joking about my sperm-count. What I'm less happy about is being a geriatric at the school gates and told how nice being a grandfather must be.

See you very soon, with all my love, for ever,

Tom.

PS I'm afraid it *is* true I told your churchy neighbours I was a lapsed mormon. But it did save you having to invite them to tea.

PPS I miss bringing tea for you tousled and naked in the morning. You smell like a warm puppy.

T.

British Embassy
Madrid

July 9th

Dear Harry,

This is not the easiest letter to write, and I hope you will bear with me as an old friend.

This morning I gave serious thought to resigning from the service and seeking admission to some kindly monastery. Having then found my mind dwelling on whether such an establishment might produce good wine, I reflected that perhaps I should not view my predicament quite so tragically. None the less I feel entirely shattered and not a little humiliated – a dunce who should be stood in the corner.

In short, it transpires that Angelica has not been what she seems. Her purity was of my own inventing. Your salacious observations from across the Atlantic were nearer the mark than they had any right to be. It appears that a fair proportion of young Madrid has tested its manhood on her with conspicuous success, not to speak of at least one member of the Royal Shakespeare Company.

How can one be so deluded? I have never before thought of myself as naive, or specially virtuous. Yet to my great discomfort I realise that buried within me lay a longing to cherish an ideal female beauty, and to treasure it as I might a piece of fine porcelain. For this absurdity I am now suffering the pain of hideous disillusionment. Your friend Tom Brand described me as a 'pin-striped Malvolio', and I'm afraid he may be right.

What I have inflicted on my beloved Ruth I scarcely

dare contemplate. And now I have driven her away: I have no idea where. She has been patience itself. A stoic. She could have sought revenge by taking any number of lovers, and she has not. On the contrary, she has devoted her lonely hours to charitable works, which have earned her much affection and acclaim. Hers is the virtue I ought to have been cherishing, not the painted simulacrum I chose instead. I feel mortified, all but destroyed by the thought of what I have done to the woman I love and no longer deserve. Ruth is warm-blooded and passionate: I am as cold as a reptile and should sleep under a stone, certainly not in a marriage bed.

If I believed there was the smallest chance of repairing what I have smashed I would seize it. But what can I possibly offer her? I am a shell; the contents have been eaten away. And that is no gift for anyone, least of all a wife. I must make a quiet exit by the back-door.

I shall be leaving this post in a matter of weeks. My successor is already here. Where I may be sent next is still undecided. If there is a consulate on the Galapagos Islands I may apply: reptiles are welcome there, so I understand. I imagine Ruth will return to London.

In any case I shall require a refresher course on bachelorhood from you. I have some leave due to me, and may beard you in Washington.

As ever,
Yours,
Piers.

93 Avenida de Cervantes
Madrid

July 10th

Dear Janice,

I need to decide whether a sense of humour is my refuge or my salvation. Three of my One Hundred Days to go, and suddenly I've won – and lost. I've routed tweetie-pie, and yet when I turn round to celebrate I find Piers in full flight in the opposite direction. I'm left standing on the battlefield all alone. Do I laugh or cry?

A quick re-cap. I am in hiding *chez* Estelle, with Piers baying for my blood for casting a smear over his immaculate Angelica: it's all a dastardly plot – how could I sink so low? – don't darken my door!

Then, midday yesterday, I get a phone call from Tom. Piers, he explains, had lined up a firing-squad for him, but the bullets struck the executioner instead. 'What the hell do you mean?' I say. Apparently Tom, newshound that he is, extracted a confession from the Blessed Angelica via the Royal Shakespeare Company to the effect that the sweet child has been screwing half the men in Madrid ever since she arrived, though *not* my husband. NOT MY HUSBAND! Am I to believe that? I suppose I have to since it comes from none other than the whore's mouth.

So, what on earth has Piers been doing all these dreadful months? Tom's answer was, 'teaching the girl about paintings.' Paintings! I had to ask him to repeat that: I thought there must have been a crackle on the line. He said it again. 'Paintings.' That took some swallowing. Since when has my classically-educated husband cast an eye upon anything artistic that postdates the Old Testament, I ask myself, especially when the alternative is the prettiest and most available bimbo in all Spain?

'In that case,' I say to Tom, 'Piers has gone utterly doolally.'

He agrees, and wonders how I come to know a fine Kiplingesque word like that.

It seems that Tom, accused of hatching a filthy plot with me, simply laid the evidence before him, and the poor man crumpled; could say nothing but 'Oh my God, what a fool, what a fool'; to which Tom voiced his assent.

As I put the phone down I knew the only course was to hurry back to Madrid and take a chance on what I was going to find. Estelle, who'd nursed me through a terrible week, gave me a kiss. Luis said, 'Good luck,' and presented me with a bunch of wild flowers. Estelle also smuggled a bottle of champagne into my suitcase, which I only found when I got back.

I looked around this empty flat, bemused. So I'd done it. I'd seen off tweetie-pie. You know, I remember reading somewhere about the exhausted silence that settles after a battle. This was what the flat felt like. I looked at July's calendar girl, and having gazed at her for a while lying there orgasmic on the beach I drew a military moustache on her face, plus a few interesting appendages elsewhere. Then I raised two fingers at her. Victory was mine.

But was my marriage mine? I realised that I'd never thought about what might happen if I actually won.

I waited for Piers to return from the embassy that evening, not having the slightest idea what to expect. Craven? Joyful? Crusty? Mad? When he did come in it was so quietly I scarcely knew he was there. He just slid in. We gazed at one another in silence. I say 'gazed at', but he seemed to be looking right through me as if I wasn't there. It was frightening. I might have been married to a ghost. It was as though he'd died and sent his shadow along to tell me so. He kept shaking his head, still looking through me. I tried to take his hand, but he froze away. I wanted to cry, but I couldn't. And he went on shaking his head. It was like an invisible screen around him, and I couldn't penetrate it.

I tried gentle persuasion. I tried reason. I tried alcohol. But all I got was a shipwrecked stare and a mumbled, 'I'm not fit for human consumption.' So I tried anger: 'Here you are, you fucking bastard, my life's been made a misery because of you for God knows how many months, and now you give me all this self-pitying crap when I'm the one you should be concerned about.' But that only made it worse: 'I *am* concerned about you; that's why I've got to leave, give you a chance of a proper life; you'll find someone better' – and all that shit.

I've never really understood masochism, not being that way inclined myself; but I realised, listening to Piers drooling on, that it's actually a form of arrogance – 'Look at me making you pay for my suffering.'

Sod you, Piers, I thought. I'm *not* going to pay for your suffering as well as my own. And I hurled a reading-lamp at him. It missed and went straight through a window-pane. There was an awful silence in the street below. The lady with the knickers appeared at the window opposite. And I burst into tears.

Piers couldn't even comfort me then. I think his battery's gone: there's no life left in him. Then, just as he'd come in as a ghost he went out as a ghost – a tormented spirit taking itself for a walk. I thought he might never come back. But he did, and went straight to bed without even a 'Goodnight'.

So I sat down and wrote this letter to you. And now I shall go out too; but not being a ghost I intend to make for the nearest bar. Over a midnight brandy I shall remind myself that there are people in this world who lead more or less normal lives. You know, for so long I assumed that Piers and I did too. But present pain forces you to re-examine past happiness, and to ask yourself, 'Was it really so happy, or were we pretending, knowing we were still young?' Hitting forty jolts men out of their dreams of being Adonis, and maybe Piers has been dreaming longer than I knew. Our most absurd vanities contain a terrible potency, and I suppose my own may rise and grab me by the throat when I too am forty.

Meanwhile, what am I to do? I joke, as always, but the clown's make-up cracks and runs. I think I know that if tomorrow is just the same there is something I must do – tear up the script, pull down the curtain, or whatever. I can't go on with this lunacy any longer, and need to find sanity somewhere.

So, Janice, I shall have my midnight brandy and gaze at the stars, wondering what I am going to find of my life in the morning.

I wish I knew a powerful god to pray to.

With much love,

Ruth.

A different bar
Madrid

July 11th

My darling Janice,

I thought my final letter before returning home should be one to remember.

Spanish tabloids probably don't reach London W4, so here's this morning's offering – just the front page, which is enough. You'll recognise the face at least; the remainder is familiar only to my imagination, for all your suspicions.

I assume it must be the first time the wife of one of Her Britannic Majesty's Chargés d'Affaires has appeared entirely naked before the eyes of the world, though perhaps some of those early colonists who 'went native' may have divested themselves on tribal occasions. Certainly, when I wrote in my article about Ruth as a leader of fashion in Madrid, this wasn't quite what I had in mind.

How it happened I have no idea, nor how our temporary Head of Mission may receive it. As far as Ruth is concerned it may be 'mission completed', I imagine; in which case it's quite an exit. It may even ensure Piers a happy posting to the Marquesas Islands, which would be a great more than he deserves, and he wouldn't need a dress allowance for his lady-wife.

Looking forward immensely to seeing you on Friday – in a not dissimilar state, I trust.

Meanwhile – all my love,

Tom.

Palacio Pizarro
Trujillo

July 11th

Dear Ruth Conway,

You must do nothing so foolish. It is no shame whatever to be seen in public as nature intended, provided of course that nature had good intentions, which in your case is abundantly clear.

On the other hand I do appreciate that you might have preferred your display not to be on the front page of that particular newspaper: the printing is crude and the readership worse.

I am afraid your early phone-call this morning caught me unawares: I had no idea what you were talking about. Fortunately Luis had a copy and recognised you at once, even though you never desported yourself quite so freely when you were here, which I always attributed to a mixture of Anglo-Saxon reserve and habits formed by your abominable climate. I am sure I would find it uncongenial to be naked in an Atlantic gale.

Firstly, I need to pay you a compliment for possessing a most enviable body. Several telephone calls have already reached me from well-wishers who know I am acquainted with you. Two or three members of the Cabinet volunteered their approval, as did a spokesman for His Highness; while the Bishop of Guadalupe, a renowned connoisseur, compared you favourably with Sophia Loren (who personally I always found a trifle vulgar). Luis, needless to say, was enthusiastic to such a degree that I have felt compelled to banish him to his wife for a few days as a punishment. No, make no mistake, you are truly Juno reborn; and all Spain loves a goddess.

As to your determination to flee the country, permit me to deter you. It is not in the least true that exposure of this kind makes you a 'marked woman', as you put it. You need to remember that a photograph of this nature arouses desire in men and envy in women: in both cases attention is focused on anatomy rather than visage. And since in the course of normal social life those areas of anatomy are clothed, it stands to reason that there is no danger of you being recognised. On the one occasion when something similar happened to me – this was in Washington many years ago – I recall many intimate friends asking me if I knew the beautiful woman in question, though it is true that the gentleman with whom I was photographed resigned from office shortly afterwards during a rather messy divorce suit. But that was entirely different: politicians are public figures, and there are certain things a public figure should never do in public.

Now – the 'culprit' in your words. Again I believe you are quite mistaken. I well remember your friend Tom Brand, he once wrote a most perceptive article on my work for Children in Need. And from my recollection of him I would never imagine him to be the type of person to have indulged in idle gossip. I am not acquainted with the place you call 'El Vino's', nor its reputation. But here in Spain 'leaks' are for politicians or plumbers, not good journalists. The notion of '*In El Vino Veritas*' strikes me as amusing but absurd.

I believe you need look no further than my amorous nephew for the 'leak'. Esteban has a somewhat unsatisfactory brother who is a photographer of sorts, and makes an uncertain living as what the Italians call a *paparazzo*: I am sure you are aware of that particular calling. I have endured the attentions of *paparazzi* on numerous occasions: they are the pirates of the illiterate press.

The most likely answer is that prior to your weekend at the hacienda my nephew made an unwise boast of his imminent conquest in the presence of his brother, who then acted on this information in the style of his profession. In my opinion there can be no other solution. It strengthens my conviction that in future we must find you a more reliable companion, to which end I continue to make strenuous enquiries. One man I particularly favour – of an excellent family – is about to be seconded to Delhi, which might prove tiresome for weekends. On the other hand I am assured by Xavier that his appointment can be postponed at least for the duration of your husband's term of office here in Spain. The man has excellent credentials and – to judge from his wife – excellent taste. I am not proposing to show him your photograph in today's newspaper: I believe such intimate revelations are best kept for the right occasion. I can also assure you that his estate is far too well guarded for any *paparazzi* to obtain access. He also has an excellent cellar: I supply it.

By the time you receive this letter I should be awaiting Xavier's arrival to take me to Madrid. I detest the place, as you well know, but as a Frenchwoman I am anxious to see for myself what your Royal Shakespeare Company makes of a French classic which has always been very close to my heart, and indeed to my life. I am told the young man who plays the Vicomte de Valmont is unusually beautiful. I confess this is another reason for my visit.

So we shall meet again very soon. Your presence in the metropolis will greatly relieve its tedium. Perhaps it can be arranged that your husband is elsewhere: with all respect to your extraordinary loyalty, I prefer not to meet other women's husbands except as lovers, and from your account of Mr Conway I doubt if he would please me in that role, and perhaps you would not wish it if he did.

Above all, I urge you to cast today's newspaper from your mind. Tomorrow another lady will grace the front page, doubtless of less generous endowment and certainly of lesser beauty.

You have become a very dear friend. Should you 'flee the country' my life would be the poorer. Kindly do not.

With my fondest regards, and deep respect,

Estelle.

93 Avenida de Cervantes
Madrid

July 13th

Dear Janice,

I clearly remember saying to you a couple of days ago that if nothing happened tomorrow I didn't believe I could go on with this lunacy any longer.

Well, it did happen! Tom has undoubtedly told you. But the unexpected also happened. Today my One Hundred Days are up, and in the cool light of dawn I believe against all the odds that I may have won my Waterloo.

The day began with Teresa coming in clutching a morning paper and looking embarrassed. '*Señora*,' was all she could utter. She slid it across the table at me. And there I was – *all* of me. Front page. And standing behind me, in riding-gear, Esteban, gazing at me like a triumphant Adonis. No woman ever looked more fucked.

For a moment I just stood there. I managed not to scream. Piers was still asleep. In a fit of panic I hid the paper under a cushion. A fat lot of use that was: what about the X-million other copies even now being drooled over, I thought? The embassy staff. All those wives. All those people I'd raised money from. Faces kept appearing before my eyes. Government ministers. Bishops. Xavier. The entire cast of the Royal Shakespeare Company. The little man I buy groceries from. Every café-owner in Madrid. Everyone I'd ever met – been at school with, had affairs with. They all had the same expression – horror.

I wasn't just naked. I was stripped. Picked clean. Flayed.

I wrenched the paper from under the cushion and had a second look. Perhaps it was some tart who just happened to look like me, and this time it would be quite obvious. It *was* quite obvious. It was me. Even the caption said so: 'The shapely wife of the British Chargé d'Affaires on holiday with Don Esteban Pelayo . . .'– it didn't say where. I knew where. It could only have been at the hacienda that weekend, and for a moment I felt a wave of relief that at least the photo wasn't of me sprawled across a Tarta de Santa Teresa or waving Esteban's dong at the vultures. But then I thought – that's just the one they chose to print; what about all the others, and where will they appear? The photographer could have sold them anywhere. *Playboy*? *Men Only*? *Boobs Galore*? *The Bethnal Green Argus*? Then my mother will see them!

I wanted to die.

Instead I made a hysterical call to Estelle, then dashed out of the flat. I hardly knew what I was doing, but I do remember hurrying along the Gran Via with a scarf wrapped across my face like a yashmak, and every time I passed a paper-stall I'd see my own breasts thrusting out at the whole world. And I'd reach over and try to slide them under a pile of *El Pais* or the *New York Herald Tribune*. I even ripped one copy off a news-stand, but the man yelled at me and I was forced to buy the bloody thing while everyone stood around gawping. And then I didn't know what to do with it. I quickly folded it the other way so it showed some footballer, and stuffed it into a refuse basket; but it developed a life of its own, and as I hurried away the paper did a sort of jump, reconstituted itself and blew across the road amid the rush-hour traffic, with my boobs cannoning off hub-caps until two boys retrieved the paper on the far side and ran off with a whoop, making balloon-like gestures with their hands.

I reached the British Embassy. It was still quite early, and only the cleaners were there plus a couple of secretaries. I knew where the papers were displayed, just outside Piers' room; so I hurried over and seized the wretched thing just as the girl was folding them all neatly on the polished table. She looked surprised, but I muttered something about a crossword puzzle and turned to leave, only to run into the incumbent ambassador.

There I was, out of breath, yashmak half across my

face, hair wild, one hand grasping the offending rag, the other extended robotically in greeting. The ambassador looked at me clothed, looked down at me naked, looked up again surprised, and said 'Good morning, Mrs Conway.'

I gave up. Be brazen, I decided.

'Good morning, Mr Bough.' I held up the paper. 'I see I've made the front page again. Last time it was on all fours: this time I'm on my back. Curious, isn't it? Perhaps you and your wife would give us the pleasure of dining with us next week.'

He nodded awkwardly, trying not to look at the paper. I refolded it so that it showed the footballer.

'Do you enjoy football, Mr Bough?' I said.

He managed a bleak smile. I hurried out of the embassy and collapsed into the first café.

I stayed there a long time trying to comb my thoughts into some sort of order. Around me all Madrid was going to work. It was nine o'clock. And no one recognised me; no one at all. And that included Piers.

I suppose I should have guessed this was the way he'd walk to the embassy: Piers has always scorned the idea of an official car, convinced that a twice-daily intake of lead-poisoning is good for his health. And there he was, striding along the pavement in one of those museum-piece linen suits Englishmen believe to be appropriate for foreign summers. He didn't look like a man who'd just seen a photograph of his naked wife splashed across the front page. A moment later I realised I was about to witness the moment when he did.

There was nothing I could do. The news-stand was perhaps fifteen yards from where I was sitting, masked behind owl-sized dark glasses. I'd been too bewildered until then to notice a fat pile of the offending newspaper displayed on a trestle-table in front of the stand. I saw Piers glance at it as he passed, take three more paces, and stop. It was as though he'd hit a wall and rebounded. His head did a half-turn like clockwork. Then his body followed, and finally his feet. The neck craned towards the pile of newspapers, gradually drawing the rest of him towards it. I saw him fumble for his spectacles and put them on. I shrank further behind my dark glasses, wishing I had a newspaper to raise in front of me. Well, I did of course, but only the one with me on it, so that was no use.

It seemed an age before he reached in his pocket for some change and actually bought the bloody thing. I imagined he'd hastily fold it to show the footballer, and then do something frantic like hail the first passing taxi or run berserk down the street.

But he didn't. He just stood there – looking at *me.*

There's an expression people have when they're very tired but there's something they urgently need to say before they sleep. Piers had that expression: I've seen it before when he's received a sudden shock. It's as though his childhood has crept up on him, and the world is too big a place.

He went on standing there for a moment or two. Then, as he started to walk away I noticed a curious thing happen. The crumpled suit seemed to fill out; his shoulders straightened; you could almost say that he strode. There was no doubt in my mind at all: I was watching a man suddenly revived, invigorated. Whatever the shock of seeing his wife unexpectedly naked in print, the result was dynamic. I removed my dark glasses and watched him disappear into the crowd of passers-by. There goes a man with a purpose, I said to myself. And what might that purpose be? Murder?

I went home.

I thought he might ring from the embassy, but he didn't. Presumably the new ambassador would have told him of our friendly encounter, and my bizarre invitation to dinner. The embassy telephone must have been buzzing even more hotly than when I opened my mouth about Gibraltar. Nobody would have been thinking or talking about anything else. Should I ring *him*, I wondered? And what would I say? I didn't. I did nothing.

About midday I was rescued by Tom. Teresa answered the phone: I was too scared. 'Meester Brand,' she said. Now I have to tell you that for a while I'd believed it might have been Tom who leaked the story of my weekend, gossiping in some journalist's bar. It was an unworthy thought, and I'd already dismissed it. So I was pleased Tom rang. He has a way of treating disasters as slightly ridiculous, and therefore blunting them.

He was laughing, the bastard. How dare he? 'I enjoyed your portrait,' he was saying. 'At last I know what I've missed all these years.'

Then he said he'd seen Piers – he'd needed some quote for a piece he was writing: not about me, he hastened to add. Now, the two of them do *not* get on. But on this occasion, Tom explained with some surprise, Piers embraced him like a friend. What should he do? What should he do? Tom suggested there wasn't an awful lot he *could* do except be thankful he was married to such a gorgeously beautiful woman and not to some flighty little bimbo. 'I know, I know,' Piers kept saying. 'It's entirely my fault.' Did Tom believe it was too late?

Well, you know Tom. 'Most probably', he said, 'but you can never be quite sure.'

Piers, he assured me, is deeply, deeply jealous. Isn't it wonderful! I've had four months of it, and now it's his turn. Wonderful!

That evening I chose to be out. Perhaps he might think I was out with my lover: I hoped so. Then, when I did come in, his eyes followed me like the eyes in a painting. Jealous, was he? How terrific. I was in heaven. I no longer gave a damn if my tits were the most exposed landmarks in the entire Spanish peninsula.

And the next day Estelle arrived, magnificently dressed like I've never seen her and preceded by a letter of splendid and whacky advice. She comes to Madrid about twice a year, and hates it. But when she's here she becomes the *marquésa.* I threw an impromptu party for her that evening, and introduced her to Tom who was leaving for London the next morning. She recognised him and they spent an hour trying to decide if they'd ever had an affair. The concensus of opinion was NO, but there were areas of doubt. 'It's so difficult to remember people when they're clothed,' Estelle announced. 'That's why I advised you, Mrs Conway, not to concern yourself over this little revelation,' she added, turning to me and brandishing the newspaper for the benefit of anyone present who might not have seen it. 'What I would have given for a body like yours, my dear. Your lover is very lucky, as well as very handsome: I shall tell him so.'

Piers was looking most uncomfortable, and a few embassy wives strenuously began to admire the view.

'This actor who plays Valmont,' she went on in a loud voice, 'is he coming?' Piers, who was standing about four feet away, turned paler still. 'I understand he has quite a reputation as a seducer – a skill I admire in a man, though he may have no need to exercise it on me: I know what I like. And so, I imagine, do quite a number of young ladies in this city.'

At this point she directed a sharp gaze at Piers.

'It always used to fall to a Chargé d'Affaires to ensure that visiting celebrities received appropriate hospitality. I imagine, Mr Conway, that you haven't neglected your duties in this respect. Female comforts do wonders for an actor's performance, off-stage and on, or so Clark Gable used to tell me. I'm sure you would agree. And you must enjoy providing a useful service. Don't we all?'

Piers felt the need to visit the loo. I detected a small smile on Estelle's lips.

'Will that do by way of settling scores?' she whispered. 'Or would you like more?'

I shook my head. Estelle left shortly afterwards for the theatre.

I had one more score to settle, and then decided against it. Esteban. After all, his snooping brother had done more than all my own well-laid plans to shake Piers out of his romantic dream. My bid for a *Playboy* centrefold may have appalled me, but it has galvanised Piers wonderfully. Besides, I owe to Esteban two 'firsts'. I can now relish the memory of being pleasured on a Tarta de Santa Teresa, *and* before an appreciative audience of vultures. And if our next posting is to be Haiti, as threatened, those memories may sustain me through a long dark night of the soul.

So – my One Hundred Days are over, and by the end of the month this Spanish sojourn will be over too. I've missed Wimbledon, and I miss you. But I know that in my heart I would have missed most of all my so-foolish and so-wise husband, who now treats me with a nervous tenderness. He asked me this morning – 'Who is this Esteban?'

Naturally I didn't tell him. I merely said, 'Certainly no angel.'

'In that case I shan't enquire where he may fear to tread,' he answered.

And his eyes had just a glint of the old Piers I love. Maybe life really is beginning to return to the corpse. Maybe I'll even feel like inviting him to see what the photographer saw. Maybe Esteban's brother will sell the remaining photos as next year's sun-tan calendar, and we shall revive our sex-life with a new surprise (in his case), and an old memory (in my case), every month.

Meanwhile, take good care of Tom. He's gold and I never knew it.

See you in London very soon. I'll drop you a note to say when.

With much love,

Ruth.

PS By the way, you wouldn't have a recipe suitable for an incumbent ambassador, I suppose? Just some tit-bit for knight starvation; nothing elaborate.

British Embassy
Madrid
July 13th

Dear Harry,

A hasty last letter before I hand over to Boring Old Fart. At this precise moment BOF is scrutinising documents I never knew existed. He has even discovered a whole new filing-cabinet: treasure-trove to the BOFs of this world.

On the domestic front, grave news. Ruth has de-cided to punish me by falling in love. Being Ruth, the form of punishment is unconventional: she has encouraged her *amour* to photograph her nude (presumably by one of those remote control devices since he is standing by her like a successful hunter), and to send the result to a disreputable Spanish tabloid. I am credited as the absent husband.

I understand the message clearly. So unfortunately does the Foreign Office. I again considered my kindly monastery.

But then a plan came to me, and I took heart. I recalled that when Napoleon Bonaparte returned from exile in Elba, his campaign lasted one hundred days. Then so shall mine, except that I shall not meet my Waterloo. My rival is youthful and undeservedly handsome; none the less I intend to defeat him by all the means at the disposal of an English gentleman, or for that matter of an English cad. Ruth is a beautiful woman and I love her.

I thought I might start by getting myself in trim. The diplomatic life is hardly conducive to an athletic build, and I have never been one for squash. Instead I shall apply myself to Ruth's discarded exercise machine –

Nautilus by name – and enjoy a daily 'work-out', if that is the correct expression. Arnold Schwarzeneggar need have no fear, but my handsome rival will.

So – One Hundred Days it is! Wish me luck.

Yours,

Piers.

PS BOF's wife closely resembles a warthog. It seems he met her in Africa. A pity it was the zoo.

1 River Mews

July 20th

Dearest Ruth,

In bewilderment, not to say panic – I've agreed to become the sixth Mrs Brand.

Tom assures me the previous five were trial runs, performed out of the kindness of his heart. He doesn't change, does he?

But I love him.

And I long to see you,

Janice.

93 Avenida de Cervantes
Madrid

July 24th

My dear Janice,

Wonderful news! Does this mean you're pregnant?

A final word on the subject of tweetie-pie. I couldn't resist a first and final visit to the British Council Library.

And from behind the bound copies of *The Illustrated London News* I distinctly overheard our new ambassador asking for books on mountaineering. Tweetie-pie was looking edible and appeared surprisingly knowledgeable on the subject, particularly once the ambassador explained who he was.

Leaning forwards, she awarded him an intimate preview of her cleavage, accompanied by a smile which Piers would know only too well.

'I've always wanted to climb in the Pyrenees,' I heard him say with feeling.

The girl reached up for a book from a high shelf, exposing a generous stretch of naked sun-tan. The jeans hung precariously on the hips.

'Perhaps you'd care to join me one weekend?' he added timorously.

Ah well, I thought, there goes another night on a bare mountain – and another loss to the diplomatic service! I wonder if he'll choose the same mountain-ledge as his predecessor. I don't imagine Piers would relish being temporary Head of Mission in Madrid a second time, do you? Although, after a few months in Haiti, who knows?

Now, tell me – when and where is the wedding? Oh Janice, we have so much to celebrate. So very much.

I'll be home almost by the time this reaches you.

Meanwhile, with much much love,

Ruth.